She didn't look like anyone's kid sister!

Where had Sam's freckles gone? Her face was pure come-hither, her mouth painted with soft lipstick, her eyes somehow bigger and more luminous.

Her eyes fastened on Tommy...delivering a sharp kick to his heart. The sultry look she was giving him simmered with sexual promises. His skin suddenly tingled from the top of his scalp to his toes. Countless times he had told himself he didn't want Sam Connelly. But this wasn't the Sam he knew. This was...

Samantha!

And if ever there was a walking invitation to discover another side of Sam, this was it!

Dear Reader,

Last year I chartered a plane to fly me from Broome, the pearling capital of the world, right across the Kimberley region of the great Australian outback. The vast plains are home to huge cattle stations, the earth holds rich minerals and the outposts of civilization are few and far between. I wondered how people coped, living in such isolated communities.

"They breed them big up here," my pilot said. "It's no place for narrow minds, mean hearts or weak spirits. You take it on and make it work." He grinned at me. "And you fly. Can't do without a plane to cover the distances."

Yes, I thought. Big men. KINGS OF THE OUTBACK. Making it work for them. And so the King family started to take shape in my mind—one brother mastering the land, running a legendary cattle station; one who mastered the outback with flight, providing an air charter service; and one who mined its riches—pearls, gold, diamonds—selling them to the world.

Such men needed special women. Who would be their queens? I wondered. They have come to me, one by one—women who match these men, women who bring love into their lives, soul mates in every sense.

I now invite you to share the journeys of the heart for these KINGS OF THE OUTBACK. This is Tommy and Samantha's story. Jared's will come next in *The Pleasure King's Bride*, on-sale August 2000, #2122. These romances encompass the timeless, primitive challenge of the Australian outback, and a touch of what the Aboriginals call "The Dreamtime."

With love,

Emma Darcy

Emma Darcy

THE PLAYBOY KING'S WIFE

Kings of the
Outback

HARLEQUIN®

TORONTO • NEW YORK • LONDON
AMSTERDAM • PARIS • SYDNEY • HAMBURG
STOCKHOLM • ATHENS • TOKYO • MILAN • MADRID
PRAGUE • WARSAW • BUDAPEST • AUCKLAND

ISBN 0-373-12116-4

THE PLAYBOY KING'S WIFE

First North American Publication 2000.

Copyright © 2000 by Emma Darcy.

This edition published by arrangement with Harlequin Books S.A.

® and TM are trademarks of the publisher. Trademarks indicated with ® are registered in the United States Patent and Trademark Office, the Canadian Trade Marks Office and in other countries.

Visit us at www.eHarlequin.com

Printed in U.S.A.

CHAPTER ONE

A KING family wedding…but it wasn't hers and Tommy's as she'd dreamed of so many times.

Even as Samantha Connelly told herself it was a terrible thing to envy people she really liked and wished well, the feeling would not go away. In another hour or so, Miranda Wade would be exchanging marriage vows with Nathan King, their love for each other would be shining out of them, and Sam just knew she was going to be sick with envy.

The worst of it was, there was no way to avoid seeing this wedding through at close quarters. As the one and only bridesmaid, she couldn't wander off and lose herself amongst the crowd of guests. She had to be on hand, performing her duties as helper of the bride, and the whole time she would have to suffer being linked to Tommy King, Nathan's brother and best man, wishing she was the bride and he was the groom.

Tommy…who still treated her like a kid sister to be petted and teased and taken for granted as a background part of his life.

Tommy…who'd probably be eyeing off every attractive woman at the wedding. But not her. Never her. And she'd end up saying something mean and bitchy to him out of sheer frustration, when what she truly wanted…

5

A knock on her door and Elizabeth King's call, "Are you dressed, Sam? May I come in?" forced a swift change of expression from gloom to the expected pleasurable excitement.

"Yes. I'm ready," she replied, preparing herself for the all too discerning scrutiny of Tommy's mother.

Elizabeth stepped into the room that had been allotted to Sam years ago when she'd first come to work on the great cattle station of King's Eden. Those days were long gone, but the sense of being at home here with Elizabeth filling the role of her stand-in mother still lingered. Comfortable familiarity and affection poured into both their smiles as they viewed each other in their wedding finery.

"You look wonderful, Elizabeth." Sam spoke first, admiring the graceful silvery grey tunic and long skirt the older woman wore with distinction. The outfit was made of a soft, fine knit and trimmed with satin ribbon, and it was set off with the beautiful pearls she always wore. Even in her sixties Elizabeth King was still a very handsome woman, tall, white-haired, with the brilliant dark brown eyes Tommy had inherited.

"So do you, Sam," came the warm reply. "More beautiful than I've ever seen you."

The compliment stirred a self-deprecating laugh. "The miracle of cosmetics. I hardly recognise myself. No freckles on show, my hair done up…" She turned to her reflection in the dressing-table mirror. "It's like looking at a stranger."

"That's because you've never bothered making

the most of yourself,'' Elizabeth commented dryly, walking over to stand behind her. Their eyes met in the mirror. ''Sometimes it does a woman's heart good to see herself at her best.''

Would Tommy see her as sexy and beautiful today? Sam wryly wondered. The lilac satin strapless gown certainly emphasised every curve of her figure. Not that she was lushly curved like Miranda. All the same, she was generally satisfied with the shape of her body and it was in proportion to her average height. The slim-line gown gave her an elegance she'd never attached to herself before, but sexy?

''Well, at least I can't be seen as a tomboy in this dress,'' she commented, trying to ease the tight, hopeless feeling in her chest.

''You shouldn't *feel* like one, either. Why not let yourself enjoy being a woman today? Don't fight it. Just let this image you see in the mirror take over and be you,'' Elizabeth quietly advised.

''But it's not really me. All this clever make-up...''

''Brings out the lovely blue of your eyes and highlights the fine bone structure of your face.''

''I've never worn my hair like this.''

Sam tentatively touched the copper curls that had been raked back and pinned into a crown around the top of her head. Usually they dangled in a mop around her face, hiding her ears and her feelings, when she needed to hide them. This style left her without any protection.

And she wasn't at all sure of the wisdom of wearing the artificial lilac rose, pushed into one side of the high nest of curls which Sam suspected would spring out and escape the pins sooner or later. However, this look was what Miranda wanted and she was the bride, so Sam had kept her mouth firmly shut while the hairdresser had done what Miranda had directed.

"Can't you see how elegant it is?" Elizabeth appealed. "Just for once your face isn't dwarfed by a riot of curls around it, and having your hair up bares the line of your neck and shoulders, showing off your milky skin."

It made Sam feel *very* bare, especially with the strapless dress, and she simply wasn't used to *elegant*, which made her very nervous about having to carry it off. What if the rose fell out and her curls tumbled down? She could just see Tommy laughing at her as the elegant sham came apart.

"It's just not me," she repeated with an apprehensive sigh, thinking she was bound to forget the eye make-up and smudge it. Probably end up looking like a clown. Especially if she wept at the wedding ceremony and the mascara ran.

"It *is* you." Elizabeth grasped her arms and looked, for a moment, as though she wanted to shake her, but she took a deep breath and contented herself by forcing Sam to hold still and keep looking in the mirror. "It's the *you* that might have been if you hadn't been brought up on an Outback cattle station, always competing with the men, trying to prove you were as good, if not better, at everything they did, from breaking in horses to mustering by helicopter."

A flush of denial scorched Sam's cheeks. "I

wasn't trying to be a man, Elizabeth. I just wanted respect from them."

"Well, maybe you were so busy winning respect, you forgot men want that, too." She sighed and her mouth curled into an ironic smile. "You were always hell-bent on proving you could beat them at their own game, even to breaking in that maverick stallion Tommy wanted to break in for himself."

Sam frowned at the criticism which had never been levelled at her before. Her recollection of that same incident was different. She'd been eighteen at the time and desperate to win Tommy's admiration and turn their relationship into something warmer, more personal.

"He was going the wrong way about it," she said in mitigation of her actions, too sensitive about her unrequited feelings to lay out her motives. "That horse didn't want to be dominated."

"So you showed him," came the pointed reply.

Her flush deepened painfully as she remembered Tommy's furious reaction to her triumphant pleasure in presenting the gentled horse. "I wasn't trying to beat him. I meant it as a gift," she muttered defensively. "I thought he'd be pleased."

Elizabeth shook her head over the lack of understanding, and with sympathy in her eyes, explained, "Tommy has been competing against Nathan all his life. It's why he broke away from Nathan's authority over the cattle station and built up his air charter business. To become his own man. Which he demanded Nathan acknowledge and respect when he asked for a portion of King's Eden to be turned into a wilderness resort for tourists.''

She paused, then shot home the truth as she saw it. ''Tommy doesn't want a woman competing with him, Sam. He wants a woman who will partner him. A woman...''

Sam bit her lip and swallowed the fiery retort that had leapt to her tongue, blitzing Elizabeth's view of what her second son wanted.... *Tommy's taste in women ran to nothing more than male ego-pumpers, not possible partners, and if he'd wanted a real partner in all his enterprises, a helpmate, a soul mate, there was none more capable and willing than she was and he was a fool for not seeing it.*

The blistering thoughts left an awkward silence after Elizabeth had stopped saying whatever she had said. Sam didn't know if some comment was expected of her. She had none to make anyway. None Elizabeth would want to hear.

With a sigh, Elizabeth released her hold and fossicked in the silver bag hanging from her wrist. ''I've brought you Nathan's gift for being Miranda's bridesmaid.'' She lifted out a purple velvet box and set it on the dressing-table.

Sam wrenched her mind out of its dark brooding and stared down at the box. No one had ever given her jewellery. A new horse, a new saddle, a motorbike, helicopter-flying lessons... all the birthday presents she'd ever requested had been aimed at what she wanted to do with her life, not at embellishing her femininity.

''I wasn't expecting anything,'' she half protested.

"It's traditional for the groom to thank the bridesmaid this way," Elizabeth explained.

"Well, never having been a bridesmaid..." She opened the box somewhat nervously, hoping Nathan hadn't spent a lot of money on her, and gasped at the beautiful pearl pendant on a fine gold chain, accompanied by matching pearl earrings. "I can't accept this!"

"Nonsense! It's the perfect complement for your dress." Elizabeth removed the delicate necklace and hung it around Sam's throat, proceeding to fasten it there.

"My ears aren't pierced." She'd tried it once in an attempt to compete with the procession of Barbie doll women Tommy favoured, but it had been a miserable failure, the holes getting badly infected, despite her taking every care.

"They're clip-ons," Elizabeth informed her. "Made especially for you. Put them on, Sam. I want to see the complete effect."

Realising argument would be futile since Elizabeth had probably chosen the set herself, Sam fumbled them onto her almost nonexistent earlobes and tried to shut her mind to what such lustrous pearls would cost a normal buyer. To the King family it wouldn't be so much, with their ownership of the pearl farm in Broome, not to mention mining interests in gold and diamonds, as well as their legendary stake in the cattle industry and Tommy's enterprises.

Their wealth had never bothered her, never really touched her...until now. She'd always earned her keep at King's Eden, working on the cattle station and in more recent years, at Tommy's resort. Still, if this was Nathan's idea of a gift for her, a memento of his wedding and the part she played in it, there really was no other option but to accept it.

"Perfect!" Elizabeth declared, her dark eyes twinkling intense satisfaction as Sam lowered her hands, revealing this fabulous last polish to her appearance. "You have such dainty ears. You should show them off more."

"Pixie ears," Sam replied with a grimace, remembering the teasing she'd suffered at school. "These earrings will probably kill me by the end of the day."

"Ah, but they set off your face and neck beautifully. Leave them on. You look absolutely perfect now. Luminous and alluring."

She would never have attached such words to herself, yet the pearls did make a difference, adding a glow that seemed to make the lilac satin and even her copper hair more lustrous.

"The beautician should be finished with Miranda in another ten minutes," Elizabeth said, checking her watch. "Better go along to her room then. She'll need help with her dress and veil. I'm just going to check on Nathan and Tommy. Make sure they're on schedule."

She was at the door before Sam found wits enough to say, "Thank you for…for everything, Elizabeth."

Her eyes locked onto Sam's once more. "Promise me…" She hesitated, grimaced. "I guess it's too much to ask."

"Please…ask."

A heavy sigh. Her eyes softened, pleading for un-

derstanding. "Don't take this unkindly. I mean it for
the best, believe me. I don't think anyone enjoys the
bickering that goes on between you and Tommy. He
baits, you bite. You bait, he bites. Do you think you
could let all that ride today? Nathan's wedding day?
I know it's a habit you've got into but it's childish
and I wish…"

She shook her head, pained at having to make the
apologetic request. Then with an earnest look and an
appealing smile, she added, "The elegant woman I
see before me doesn't have to compete with anyone.
Carry that thought with you, Sam. Win respect…for
being a woman."

Childish…The accusation burned through Sam for
several minutes after Elizabeth had left. The worst of
it was having to acknowledge the tit-for-tat game had
started in their teens, probably a childish bid on her
part to gain and hold Tommy's attention. But it had
been fun in those days. It hadn't developed bite until
after the horse-breaking incident, his furious resentment of her action stirring resentment in her. And
sickening disappointment.

Since then…ten years of bickering, with the pattern of behaviour between them so deeply set, Sam
didn't know if she could stop it. In some perverse
way, it had felt like a bond of intimacy between
them, a running commentary on each other's lives
that none of his simpering women could share because it went so far back and held so much familiarity…

But she didn't *want* to be his kid sister.

With despairing anguish clutching her heart, Sam

turned to look again at the woman in the mirror. Not one trace of a childish spitfire in that woman. Elegant, luminous, alluring...could she be *her* today? Would Tommy treat her differently, see in her a woman he wanted in his bed, making love instead of making war?

Sam took a deep breath and made a fierce resolution.

Today, no matter how hard it might be to keep it up, she would be that woman, inside and out. She would hold that image in her mind and live up to it. Not because Elizabeth had asked her to. Not because it was Nathan's wedding. Because suddenly, she saw it as her only hope to change the ground between her and Tommy, and if it didn't work...perhaps nothing ever would.

CHAPTER TWO

HAD SHE been too hard?

Elizabeth fretted over the question as she headed towards Nathan's quarters. She had never considered Sam fragile, more a fighter, a survivor against any odds, always bouncing back with a stubborn determination to win out in the end. But she was fighting the wrong fight with Tommy. And sometimes, Elizabeth firmly told herself, one had to be cruel to be kind.

All the same, it troubled her that Sam had looked so...*vulnerable.* Somehow it evoked the sense of its being make or break time for these two—the son who could always make her laugh and lift her spirits, and the child-girl-woman who'd become a thorn in his side instead of the smile in his heart. What should have turned out right for both of them had taken a wrong twist and Elizabeth wasn't sure if her interference could correct it.

After years of observing them at loggerheads, she had come to the conclusion that pride wouldn't allow them to change their attitudes. Maybe it was too late and the mutual sniping had killed what might have been. Laid it to waste. She'd tried to tell them, lecturing them on lost opportunities, time going past that could never be regained, but to no avail. If she couldn't jolt them into a new awareness of each other at this wedding...well, at least she would have tried.

Ultimately, they were responsible for their own happiness. The problem was—Elizabeth no longer trusted them to make it happen themselves. Not that she could make it happen, either. All she could do was push.

Nathan wasn't in his room.

Tommy's was vacant, as well.

She found all three of her sons sitting at the bar in the billiard room, Jared, her youngest, pouring champagne into glasses. In their formal black tie wedding attire, each one of them was strikingly handsome, though quite individual in their looks; Nathan so big and tall and strong and impressively male, with the bluest of blue eyes and straight black hair, almost the image of his father; Tommy, with his endearing, untameable tight black curls, and wickedly charming brown eyes, always the flash of a mischievous devil about him; and Jared, having a less obvious strength, a quieter charm, his eyes darkly serious and always receptive, just a wave in his black hair, subtly providing a balance between the other two.

For several moments Elizabeth stood still, enjoying her pride in them. Lachlan would be proud of them, too, she thought, wishing her husband was still alive and at her side today, celebrating the wedding of his firstborn. His boys were all men now, men in their own right and pursuing their chosen paths, and it did Elizabeth's heart good to see them so happily at ease with each other, enjoying a togetherness they rarely had time to share.

"I thought you would have all had more than enough to drink at last night's buck's party," she remarked, finally drawing their attention.

"Just a last toast to the end of my bachelorhood," Nathan excused with a grin.

"Settling his nerves," Jared teased.

"I, for one, definitely need fortification," Tommy declared. "Any man who partners Sam has to be fighting fit, and since I've been elected..."

"You could give it a break, Tommy," Nathan suggested. "Treat Sam like a lady instead of a sparring partner. Then she'd have nothing to hit off."

Elizabeth flashed her eldest son a grateful look, pleased to have a ready ally.

"Sam, a lady?" Tommy's mouth curled into a mocking smile. "First, she wouldn't know how to respond. Second, she'd accuse me of sending her up. Or she'd suspect me of some nefarious motive and see everything I did and said as a trap which I'd somehow spring on her when she'd most hate it."

He swept out an arm, gesturing to Elizabeth, his eyes beaming warm admiration. "Now, there you see a real lady. And may I say you look wonderful, Mum. Doing Nathan proud today."

"Thank you, Tommy. And I happen to think Samantha will do you proud...if you let her."

"Samantha?" His eyebrows shot up. "Since when has Sam become Samantha?"

"You'll see," Elizabeth replied knowingly, piquing curiosity.

"A glass of champagne for you, Mum?" Jared asked.

"No, thank you. I just came to check that you're all ready and nothing's amiss."

"Do we pass inspection?" Nathan asked with an amused, confident smile.

For a moment, he reminded her so strongly of Lachlan on their wedding day, she choked up, nodding her approval to cover the emotional block.

"What am I going to see?" Tommy drawled, his voice laced with scepticism. "Has Miranda waved some magic wand over Sam?"

"Could I have a private word with you, Tommy?" Elizabeth asked.

"I've got the ring." He patted his trouser pocket. "I know all the duties of a best man. You can trust me to carry them out. And despite whatever barbs Sam chooses to sling at me, my speech thanking the bridesmaid will be all you'd want it to be. Does that cover it?"

"Not quite. Please…just a few minutes of your time," Elizabeth insisted, gesturing to the adjoining lounge room.

With a much put-upon roll of his eyes, he heaved himself off the bar stool, then wickedly broke into a song and dance. "'Oh, we're going to the cha-a-apel, going to get ma-a-arried…'" And to his brothers' huge merriment, swept Elizabeth into a dance hold and whirled her into the adjoining room with all the panache of the playboy image he'd cultivated.

And what did that cover? Elizabeth had often wondered. She didn't believe he had a lust for many women. To her mind, it was more a restless search for someone to answer needs that Sam wouldn't or couldn't answer. Or a pride thing, proving other women found him readily desirable. But it wasn't giving him what he truly wanted. Elizabeth was certain of that.

"So..." he said, bringing her to a halt beyond ready earshot of the others. "...what's on your mind?"

She caught her breath, wishing she didn't have to dampen the devilish twinkle in his eyes. But she loved Tommy too much to let him hide his deep-down needs behind a wall of frivolous fun.

"It's Nathan's wedding day," she started.

He made a mock frown. "I truly am aware of that fact."

"Yes...well, I'd like it to be a very happy occasion. No bickering or snide little cracks."

He raised his eyebrows in a show of innocence. "I am the very soul of pleasure on tap."

"Then show that soul to Samantha for once, Tommy. You heard Nathan. He won't ask it directly of you but I shall. Give the fighting a break. Be kind, generous..."

His face closed up.

"Tommy, I am just asking you to treat her as you would any other woman. Don't mess this up."

"Mess what up?" he demanded coldly.

"This day. You're older than she is. And God knows you've had enough experience of women to handle the situation with finesse. She's nervous. She's afraid..."

"Afraid?" His eyes flashed derision. "Sam's never been afraid of anything."

"You think I'm a fool, Tommy? You think I'm just talking to hear myself speak?"

He glanced away, breath hissing out between his teeth.

"I'm telling you she doesn't have her usual armour today," Elizabeth drove on. "I'm telling you she's vulnerable. And if you hurt her, Tommy…it would be very, very wrong."

"I have no intention of hurting Sam," he grated.

She reached out and squeezed his arm. "I hope you take very great care not to. For your sake. And hers," she said quietly.

His gaze swung back, eyes blazing a fierce challenge. "You think it's all my fault?"

The banked passion behind those words told Elizabeth more than Tommy had ever told her…the long-burning frustration of his relationship with Samantha Connelly. But there was nothing to be gained by placing blame anywhere. Raking over the past wouldn't help. She had to appeal to the man he was now, the man who still wanted what could be…if the ground was shifted.

"No," she answered, her eyes holding his with love and understanding. "I simply trust you're big enough…and I know you are, Tommy…to rise above it today. To give of yourself without asking or expecting a return or a reward. Just to give…because giving is what today is about."

His mouth twisted into a wry smile. "Okay. You have a deal. For what it's worth." His eyes gently mocked as he added, "But you must know Sam's bound to make tatters of any gift from me."

"Then the fault will indeed be all hers. Thank you, Tommy."

"Oh, I'll be having the pleasure of being a martyred saint," he rolled out in an Irish lilt, a resurgence of devilment in his eyes.

She smiled. "Have I told you lately that I love you?"

His face softened. "You don't have to. You've always been on my side when I've needed you. And to simply say thank you is totally inadequate. But thanks all the same, Mum."

Elizabeth had never had any hesitation in throwing family money behind Tommy's enterprises, the small planes and helicopter charter business which he'd called KingAir, the wilderness resort that bore the same name as the cattle station, King's Eden, since it had once been a part of it.

He'd had a great need to prove himself, away from Nathan's big shadow, Nathan who was born to be the cattle King and wear his father's shoes. Tommy had to be his own man, and he was, very much his own man now, solidly successful in his business life.

But his personal life…he envied the love Nathan had found with Miranda. Elizabeth had seen it in his eyes on the night of their engagement party and knew he craved the same kind of love…to be accepted and respected and loved for the person he was inside.

"Let's have a happy day, Tommy," she said, knowing he would respond to her appeal for peace with Samantha.

"Sure, we will. The happiest of days. Especially for Nathan."

For you, too, Elizabeth willed. "I must go back to Miranda. Everything else is in order?"

"Running like clockwork. Don't worry. We're onto the countdown now and everything will go brilliantly."

"I hope so."

He tapped her cheek in tender affection. "It's all right. You have my promise. I'll keep smiling in the face of the tiger."

"Thank you, Tommy."

It was with a lighter heart that Elizabeth returned to the bride. She'd done what she could to set up a harmonious situation. What might come out of it was up to Tommy and Samantha now.

The bridesmaid and the best man.

A wedding.

Surely they would feel what was missing from their lives and make an effort to leap over the barriers between them and grasp this chance. Pride simply wasn't worth the loss of love.

CHAPTER THREE

At precisely 3:45, as scheduled, Tommy and Nathan stepped off the homestead verandah, leaving Jared behind to escort Miranda down the aisle in place of the unknown father who'd played no part in her life. She had no family, but she was not to walk alone. Never again alone, Nathan had sworn.

They walked down the path to where a white pergola had been erected, framing the front entrance opening. On either side of it the old bougainvillea hedge was a mass of multicoloured bloom on this fine Saturday afternoon. Shade cloth had been spread over the top of the pergola to hold off the hot sun while Miranda and Sam waited there to make their entrance. Tommy and Nathan slid out past the white lattice gates which would hide the bridal procession from view until The Moment.

A long strip of red carpet had been laid across the road, bisecting the large circular lawn in front of the homestead and leading straight to the white gazebo which had been set up at the other end of it. The whole area was shaded by magnificent old trees, the wide spread of their branches interlacing, providing the best protection for the three hundred guests, most of whom had flown in from all over Australia.

Many were already seated on the white chairs which had been laid out in a church pattern, the bulk of them facing the gazebo, but with two sections parallel to it—special sections reserved for the resort and station staff with their families on one side, and on the other, the Aboriginal tribe which had been tied to King's Eden from its beginning over a hundred years ago.

This was undoubtedly the biggest Outback wedding ever held in the Kimberly, Tommy thought, smiling to himself at the idea of another King legend in the making. There were many of them from the old days, but this…this was something else and he was proud to have had a big hand in it with KingAir flying in many of the guests and his resort providing the accommodation. Nathan couldn't have managed such a gathering on his own.

As they strode down the red carpet aisle together, a buzz of anticipation ran through the crowd. Those who hadn't taken their seats moved to settle down for the long awaited ceremony. Out of the corner of his eye, Tommy noticed Janice Findlay lingering on her feet, watching him, probably wanting his attention to turn her way.

It was over between them, as far as he was concerned, so he gave her no encouragement. He hoped she wasn't going to try reviving their affair today. The problem with Janice was she drank too much, fun when she was only tiddly but no fun at all when she bombed herself out.

If she made some kind of scene in front of Sam, the fat would be in the fire. Sam would undoubtedly let fly with caustic comments and he'd have to weather them, in keeping with his promise to his mother. He willed Janice to target some other guy at the wedding. His patience and good humour were going to be tested enough, keeping Sam sweet, though he doubted that was even remotely possible. There was no honey in her nature to start with.

Vulnerable? Well, maybe Miranda had put her in high heels and she was scared of wobbling up the aisle or tripping over herself. Sam would certainly hate looking less than competent. She probably felt like a fish out of water in female finery, having prided herself on mastering a man's world from the day she was born a girl instead of a boy.

It was to be hoped she didn't fall flat on her face. He wouldn't wish that humiliation on her, not in front of this crowd and right at the beginning of the wedding, though she was damned good at dishing out humiliation herself. Not only was she a first-class expert at one-upmanship, she nitpicked everything he did, as though she always knew better. The exasperating part was that too often she proved she was right.

Which annoyed the hell out of him.

One of these days he was going to get the better of Sam Connelly. But, given his promise to his mother, today was not the day. Unless…

A smile twitched at his lips. What if he gave her the full playboy charm treatment on this auspicious occasion…bridesmaid and best man? Shower her with compliments. Keep pressing to do whatever would make her feel happy. Focus on her needs and desires. In short—bewilder, bewitch and bedazzle.

He broke into a chuckle at the thought of clipping Sam's claws, one by one.

"What's amusing you?" Nathan asked.

"You may not be the only winner today, big brother," he answered with a grin.

Nathan looked about to pursue the point, but the pastor hailed him, breaking away from a group of guests he'd been chatting to and joining them as they reached the gazebo. With any private conversation diverted, Tommy contented himself envisaging various scenarios between him and Sam, where she would be left floundering under a barrage of unquenchable charm.

The sight of his mother emerging onto the red carpet aisle jolted his mind back onto the job of getting this wedding under way. He signalled to Albert and the other tribal elder, Ernie, to take their seats on either side of the gazebo. Out they came from amongst their families, carrying their didgeridoos—the long wooden instruments highly polished for the occasion—and with great dignity, settled themselves ready to play.

His mother reached the top of the aisle and held out her arms in a gathering gesture. With great excitement, the children streamed out from their shaded seats, all the girls under twelve years old from the station families, and two boys from the Aboriginal community. They were all puffed up with self-importance as they lined up in front of the gazebo, the boys in front, their sleek brown bodies daubed in ceremonial patterns, and both of them carrying a tribal spear, six girls in pairs behind them, looking very cute in frilly lilac dresses, white socks and shoes, little white daisies circling their hair, and carrying pretty white baskets filled with rose petals.

His mother had a few quiet words with them. There was much earnest nodding. Then off they went down the aisle, the girls positioning themselves at their allotted intervals, the boys marching straight for the white lattice gates which they were to open at the first long note from the didgeridoos. As soon as the boys were in place, his mother took her seat.

"Ready?" Tommy couldn't resist shooting at Nathan.

"Ready," he replied in a heartfelt tone.

Tommy gave the nod to Albert and Ernie, and unaccountably felt a soaring anticipation himself as the ancient Aboriginal instruments started their deep, rhythmic thrum, calling up the good spirits from the Dreamtime to bless this union with longevity and fertility. It was a sound that seemed to reverberate through the heart, linking everyone to an earthbeat as old as time itself.

In unison, the boys opened the gates wide…and out stepped…Sam?

Disbelief seized Tommy's mind.

Sam…looking like some stunning model from a fashion magazine?

A shower of rose petals dotted his vision for a moment but then she walked past them without the slightest wobble in her step. She was carrying herself straight and tall, just as his mother did. Tall? Her hair was up! The mop of bouncy red ringlets wasn't a mop anymore. It was sleeked back from her face and tamed into a sophisticated arrangement on top of her head, gleaming like burnished copper, and set off with a lilac rose nestled artistically to one side.

A brilliant touch, that rose. Made Sam look elegant and seductively feminine. And the dress she was wearing was downright sexy! Looked as though she had been poured into it, the shiny fabric emphasising a very female figure, surprisingly well-rounded breasts holding up the strapless bodice—tantalising hint of cleavage there—and a waist small enough to give a man a snug handhold, a waist that highlighted perfectly curved hips that were swaying from side to side with almost mesmerising grace.

Over her stomach she held a dainty bouquet of white daisies and green leaves, and beneath that the movement of her legs, pushing rhythmically at the shiny, slippery, slim-line skirt was incredibly sensual. Tommy started to feel the pricking of desire and a strong urge to act on it. Another shower of rose petals reminded him of where he was and the dignity required of a best man. He wrenched his gaze up from the dangerously exciting skirt.

Lovely shoulders, neck…and she was wearing pearls! A pendant gleaming on her skin below her throat and droplet earrings dangling provocatively on either side of her face. And where had her freckles gone? One thing was certain. She didn't look like anyone's kid sister!

There was nothing forbidding about that face. It was pure come-hither, her mouth painted with soft lipstick, cheekbones shaded to an exotic slant, eyebrows peaking and winging, drawing his attention to the milky smoothness of a forehead he'd never seen before, and her eyes…somehow bigger and more luminous.

Eyes fastened on him…delivering a sharp kick to his heart. The sultry look she was giving him simmered with sexual promises. His skin suddenly tingled from the top of his scalp to his toes. Countless times he had told himself he didn't want Sam Connelly. A man would have to be a masochist to want her. But this wasn't the Sam he knew. This was…

Samantha!

O-o-o-oh yes! His mother had that much right.

And if ever there was a walking invitation to discover another side of Sam, this was it, and any thought of being *lumbered* with having to do right by her or even amusing himself with games, went right out of Tommy King's mind.

CHAPTER FOUR

SAM WAS NOT sick with envy during the wedding ceremony. She was sick with excitement. The way Tommy had looked at her as she'd walked up the aisle kept buzzing through her mind and churning her insides to such a pitch she wasn't even aware that the bride and groom were up to exchanging vows over the wedding ring until Miranda turned to give Sam her bouquet to hold.

In no time at all the pastor was declaring Nathan and Miranda "Husband and Wife," and they were moving towards the table at the back of the gazebo to register the marriage in the official book and sign the certificate.

Sam's heart was thumping hard as she and Tommy followed. She couldn't bring herself to look directly at him, afraid she had read too much into his expression, and now that the surprise of her appearance was over, there might only be the usual teasing glint in his eyes.

"Quite a revelation," he murmured.

"What?" The word tripped out before she could catch it back. Desperate to know if he was baiting her, as usual, she risked a quick glance at his face.

"You in all your glory," he answered, his eyes warmly caressing, not even a twinkle of mischief.

"Miranda's choice," she mumbled, thrown into

hot confusion by his open admiration and hopelessly inept at accepting such a personal compliment.

"You grace it with high distinction," came the smooth rejoinder, his voice sounding sincere.

"Thank you," she managed this time, grateful for a second chance to give a gracious response.

He lightly grasped her elbow to steer her around behind the now seated bride. She had never felt so conscious of a touch. Was he just being gentlemanly on this formal occasion or was he wanting physical contact with her?

"You look very dashing yourself in formal wear," she said, giving in to the urge to show she could be generous, too.

"Mmmh…may I take that as a vote of approval?"

As he brought them to a halt, ready to move in as witnesses when required, she caught his quirky smile out of the corner of her eye and instantly hissed, "I'm sure you'll have every unattached woman here slathering over you in no time flat."

Before she could regret the tart remark, he leaned over and whispered, "You have my permission to beat them off."

She flinched at the tingle of his breath on her bared ear. "Why should I do that?" snapped straight off her wayward tongue, pride blowing resolution away.

"Because I'm your partner for the day."

Provoked by this dutiful stance she flashed him an arch look. "I might fancy someone else."

His eyes simmered darkly at her. "I'll beat off anyone who comes sniffing around you."

This was a far more satisfying image than her

beating women off him. Nevertheless, she couldn't stop herself from saying, "I don't want you to feel tied to me, just because you're the best man and I'm the bridesmaid."

"Ah, but I *want* to be tied to you today, Samantha."

He accompanied his soft, seductive drawl of her full name with a look that challenged everything female in her, and that same everything started quivering with delight. She hadn't fooled herself. He *was* seeing her as a desirable woman. And if she didn't stop these stupidly self-defeating reactions, she'd spoil this new view of her. Tommy was offering what she wanted, even if it was only for today, and if she didn't take it and run with it she'd be an absolute fool.

She poured all her wild hopes into a smile, desperately needing to negate her prickliness. "Then I'll be pleased to have your company, Tommy."

"I shall hold you to that," he murmured, a triumphant twinkle lighting his eyes.

Sam's heart leapt joyously at this evidence of serious intention. So lost was she in the magical possibility of secret dreams teetering on the edge of reality, she almost jumped when Nathan called to her.

"Your turn to sign," he said, rising from the table and waving her forward. He smiled, his blue eyes brilliant with inner happiness. "You make a beautiful bridesmaid, Sam."

"Doesn't she?" Miranda chimed in, turning her radiance on both Sam and Tommy.

"Ravishing!" Tommy roundly declared, nudging her forward.

"Thank you," she rushed out breathlessly, Tommy's "Ravishing!" ringing in her ears and dancing through her mind. He hovered beside her as she sat and wrote her signature where the pastor pointed and the pen wobbled on the page, her hand seemingly disconnected to the task required, trembling with the excitement coursing through her.

When she'd finished, Tommy took the pen from her, not bothering to sit down, his arm encircling her bare shoulders as he leaned over the table and scrawled his signature with swift and masterful confidence. She stared at his handsome profile, almost disbelieving the feather-light caress of his fingers on her upper arm. He'd never touched her like this, as though wanting to feel her skin. Despite the heat of the afternoon, the tingling caress was causing her to break out in goose bumps.

"There! All witnessed!" he said, reminding her of where they were and why.

She jumped up, dislodging his hold, too superconscious to let it continue. As it was, her heart was pounding erratically as she swung around to the bride and groom. There was Nathan, a strong mountain of a man, a sound and steady friend whose kindness to her at times could only have meant he knew how she felt about his brother.

Was it all right now? she wanted to ask him. Could she trust what was happening? Was this playboy stuff from Tommy or was he intent on starting a different relationship with her? No more kid sister.

Whether Nathan read the appeal right, the tormenting uncertainty in her eyes, Sam didn't know, but he gave her a reassuring smile and a nod of approval which momentarily soothed the turbulence inside her. Impulsively, she stepped over and poured her emotion into a congratulatory hug which he warmly returned.

"I hope you two have the happiest of lives together," she said with genuine fondness for the newly wedded couple, then turning to the woman who'd won his heart. "And, Miranda, you must truly be the most beautiful bride in the whole world."

"She is to me," Nathan said with such love, tears pricked Sam's eyes.

Would Tommy ever say that of her?

The photographer summoned them to stand in a group in front of the gazebo, facing the wedding guests. Remembering her bridesmaid duties, Sam checked that Miranda's veil was falling right from the single white rose fastened in the gleaming blonde chignon, and that the beaded hem of her fabulous wedding gown was displayed properly along the folds of the graceful train.

"Enough! That's perfect," Tommy murmured, scooping her with him to stand in line for the photographs.

His arm remained around her waist, coupling them very much together, and even when the photographer was satisfied with the shots he'd taken, and the pastor announced that guests could now come forward to congratulate the bride and groom, Tommy did not release his hold, drawing her aside with him, his hand applying a light pressure around the curve of her hip.

"They look great together, don't they?" he said warmly, watching his mother and Jared bestowing a kiss on Miranda and pressing Nathan's hand.

"Do you mind losing her to Nathan?" The question slipped out, voicing the long insecurity which had been fed by Tommy's interest in other women.

He frowned. "Why would you think that? I never had Miranda to lose."

Somehow Sam couldn't let it go. "You were attracted to her when she first came to manage the resort," she stated flatly.

Beautiful, elegant Miranda, with her swishing blonde hair, lushly curved body, and fascinating green eyes hiding the mystery of her private life, keeping her distance while Tommy chased...Sam had been in knots, expecting Miranda to succumb, but she never did.

He slid her a look that challenged her judgment. "Was I?"

The taunting little question spurred her to remind him, "You kept asking her out with you."

His eyes seemed to mock her knowledge of those invitations even as he sardonically replied, "Curiosity. She was in charge of my resort. I wanted to know what made her tick...a woman like that, keeping herself to herself. You were curious, too, remember? It was you who tackled her head-on about the family she never spoke about."

She flushed at the memory. "That was awful. I

was so grateful to Nathan for smoothing it over with tales of your family.''

''At the time, I backed you up, pressing the question. Simple curiosity, Samantha. I'm not attracted to cool blondes.'' His mouth curved into a slow, sensual smile. ''I'm much more drawn to a fiery combination.''

Sam's heart flipped. The flush in her cheeks deepened. She just wasn't used to Tommy turning this kind of attention on her, and as much as she had craved it, she found herself in wretched confusion as to whether it was real or not. Somehow it felt wrong that a superficial change in her appearance should spark such a difference in his behaviour towards her.

Before she could sort out her own ambivalence, her family came streaming towards her, having been close behind Elizabeth and Jared in offering their congratulations to the bride and groom. The friendship between the Kings and the Connellys went back a long way—three generations—both families running cattle stations in the Kimberly, and Sam had been the only girl born to either family in the current generation.

Three sons to Elizabeth and Lachlan.

A daughter and two sons to Robert and Theresa Connelly.

Sam reluctantly acknowledged it was true, what Elizabeth had said earlier. All her growing-up years she had wanted to be a boy—or every bit as good as a boy in her father's eyes. Until Tommy had started stirring other feelings in her, feelings that she hadn't known how to handle then. Or now.

The distraction of her family was welcome, familiar faces, people who loved her. Her father looked very distinguished in a suit, his mane of thick white hair—all red gone out of it in recent years—curling away from his still ruggedly handsome face. Strange, she had been the only one to inherit his hair and blue eyes. Her younger brothers, Greg and Pete were built like their father, but had their mother's dark colouring, and both of them looked very attractive, all brushed up for the wedding. Her mother, as always, was the essence of femininity, her dainty figure encased in a peach lace dress.

Robert Connelly's voice boomed out from his big, barrel chest. "Well, look at you!" His hands grasped Sam's arms, squaring her up for his beaming pride and admiration. "So much for your mother's accusation I was making a man of you by letting you have your head about doing what you wanted." He turned triumphantly to his wife. "My Sam can turn into a beautiful woman any time she likes."

Her mother regarded her with more whimsical bemusement. "I couldn't imagine you looking more lovely, Samantha," she said quietly. "It was like a dream, watching you walk up the aisle."

"I guess dreams can come true sometimes, Mum," Sam wryly answered, still helplessly insecure about Tommy's response to her.

They stayed chatting about the wedding for a while before spotting friends and moving away to catch up with them. Her brothers lingered to make teasing remarks to Tommy about keeping their suddenly glamorous sister under his wing. He blithely replied he was the *best man* to take care of her, and under his wing was precisely where she belonged, this claim being accompanied by a light hug, plunging her straight into more emotional and physical turmoil as the length of her body was drawn against his, her arm pressed to his chest, hip to hip, thigh to thigh.

Her brothers laughed and wished Tommy the best of luck as they drifted off in search of some luck of their own. Sam was inwardly reeling from the electric awareness of being this close to him, feeling the strong masculinity of his physique, smelling the subtly enticing cologne he must have dabbed on his neck, sensing the strong current of energy that was so much a part of his vibrant personality.

"Do you know this rose in your hair is right in line with my mouth?" he softly mused. "I have the most extraordinary urge to pluck it out with my teeth and sweep you into a wild tango."

"Don't!"

Jolted into tilting her head to look up at him, she lost the train of protest, any further words dying in her throat. His face was perilously close to hers, the smooth clear-cut line of his jaw that invited stroking, the mouth perfectly shaped for kissing, a nose that seemed to embody a flare of passion, dark eyes dancing with wickedness and fringed with thick long lashes that were sinfully seductive, eyebrows slanting into a diabolical kick and the springy black curls that made him look so dangerously rakish.

"Such appealing eyes," he murmured. "Why

have I never seen them appealing to me before, Samantha?''

Her heart was in her mouth. She couldn't answer.

''I would always have answered an appeal from you,'' he went on. ''As I will now. Your rose is safe...until you want to match me in wanting to let your hair down and...''

''Tommy!''

The sharp call of his name broke the intimate weave of his words around her heart. It was a woman's voice, claiming his attention. Sam's head jerked towards it and her stomach contracted as she saw who the woman was...Janice Findlay, Tommy's most recent flame, and flaming she was in the look she gave Sam, a scorching dismissal that left her burning.

Before today, Sam would have instantly disengaged herself and left Tommy to his playmate. Never would she have contested any woman for his attention. But it seemed to her his words had given her the right to stay at his side and how he handled this situation would tell her more of where she stood with him than anything else.

''Ah, Janice,'' he addressed her coolly, his arm hugging Sam more tightly, apparently determined on preventing her from moving away. ''Enjoying the wedding?'' he casually added, as though Janice Findlay was no more than another guest to him.

Her auburn hair came out of a bottle, Sam decided, noting the darker roots at the side parting. So much for Tommy's taste for a *fiery combination*. Nevertheless, Janice was certainly aiming to heat up the opposite sex, the low V-neckline of her slinky black dress putting her prominent breasts on a provocative display.

"It's quite unique, darling...the setting, the Outback touch with the didgeridoos...my parents thought it marvellous," she drawled in a sexy voice. "Absolutely honoured to have been invited."

"I'm glad they're having a good time." A strictly polite reply.

Undeterred, Janice offered him a smile that reeked of provocative promise. "I notice drink waiters are circulating with glasses of champers. Come and have some bubbly with me, darling. You must be dying of thirst."

"Janice, I'm sure you can find someone else to share your fondness for champagne." There was a steely note driven through the smooth suggestion, and it emphasised his stance as he added, "As you can see...I'm busy."

Even Sam caught her breath at the direct and unmistakable rejection. As much as she wanted to be put first, it seemed a cruel set-down to a woman who probably had every right to expect him to keep fancying her.

Janice's smile twisted into bitter irony. "Off with the old, on with the new, Tommy?"

"The old ended some time ago, as well you know," he retorted quietly. "Making a scene won't win you anything, Janice."

"Won't it?" Her chin tilted up belligerently, her eyes flashing fiery venom, shot straight at him, then targeting Sam. "Well, just don't think you're sitting pretty, Samantha Connelly,'' she drawled derisively. "You won't win anything, either.''

With a scornful toss of her hair, she turned her back on them and headed straight for one of the drink waiters. She snatched a glass of champagne off his tray, held his arm to stay his progress through the milling crowd, threw the drink down her throat, replaced the empty glass and grabbed another full one.

"At that rate she'll be under a table before the reception dinner begins,'' Tommy muttered in dark vexation.

"You were…rather cutting,'' Sam commented, feeling a twinge of sympathy for the woman he'd cast aside. She knew all too well the frustration of wanting Tommy King, and not being able to reach into him.

"She was unforgiveably rude in her self-serving attempt to cut you out,'' he stated tersely.

"Perhaps she felt she had just cause.''

Tommy swung her around to face him, anger blazing from his eyes. "Why do you always assume the worst of me?''

Did she? Maybe she did, in some kind of perverse bid to make him less desirable so she wouldn't want him so much. "I'm sorry. I didn't mean to,'' she rushed out in guilty agitation. "I just don't know where you're coming from, Tommy, and faced with Janice like that…''

"My involvement with Janice ended the night she did a striptease at a party, then fell on her face, dead drunk,'' he bit out in very clear distaste. "For me it was a complete turn-off. I saw her home safely but that was it. And I told her so. She has no excuse for slighting you and no cause to malign me.''

To Sam's intense relief, his expression changed, the anger swallowed up as his eyes gathered a commanding intensity. He lifted a hand and laid its palm gently on her cheek. ''Please...don't let her spoil this.''

Sam could not tear her eyes away from his though the passionate wanting they were communicating made her head swim. She snatched at her belief that Tommy was fundamentally decent, which surely meant he wasn't playing some deceitful game with her. He was speaking the truth. She just didn't know what *this* was to him.

''Give me credit, Samantha,'' he demanded, a harsh note creeping into his voice. ''I will not be robbed of respect today.''

Respect...the word sliced through the whirling doubts with all the force of Elizabeth's earlier reading of the problem she had created with Tommy, her failure to comprehend his need for respect or even what it meant to him.

Panicked at the thought of doing more wrong, she instinctively lifted her hand and covered his in a gesture of appeasement, as well as desperately seeking a sense of togetherness with him. ''I believe you,'' she blurted out, taking the leap of faith he asked of her.

The tension eased from his face. He smiled—a brilliant, dazzling smile—and Sam felt bathed in an exhilarating radiance. Her heart lightened. Her taut nerves relaxed into a melting sense of pleasure. Her mind was filled with the sunrise of a day she had yearned for. This was it…she and Tommy…with a clean slate between them.

CHAPTER FIVE

YES!

A fierce elation burst through Tommy. She'd given in to him. For once in her life she hadn't suspected his word, flouted it, mocked it, or walked away from it. And placing her hand on top of his was more than acceptance. Much more. It was a voluntary move towards him.

"Thank you," he breathed, revelling in the appeal to him in her eyes, the appeal of a woman who didn't want to fight, a woman who was looking—hoping—for something else from him, feeling her way tentatively towards it.

"I may not have said it, but I do admire all you've achieved, Tommy," she said earnestly. "The success you've made of the air charter business and the wilderness resort. They were great ideas and you've proved how timely they were with Outback tourism gathering more and more business."

The admission was surprisingly sweet. He was beyond needing anyone's approval or admiration for his pursuit of ventures he'd believed in. His own satisfaction in making them profitable was enough. But coming from his most nagging critic...

"I never meant to sound as though I always thought the worst of you," she rushed on apologet-

44

ically. "I do respect your...your judgment on these things."

Now *that* was pure grovel and he didn't believe it for a second. She'd used him as a whipping boy far too often, invariably casting him in the worst possible light. On the other hand, the attempt at conciliation was intriguing. What did *Samantha* want today?

Her earlier tart responses had denied any desire for him and she'd been tense and uncomfortable with every physical contact he'd made. But just before Janice's intrusion, he'd definitely been on a promising roll. Keep it wild, he thought, out of the ordinary.

"Shall we start over?" he suggested whimsically.

She looked confused.

He moved his hand to capture hers and carry it to his lips. "I truly am charmed to meet you, Samantha Connelly," he declared, brushing a kiss across the back of her fingers. "And I look forward to forging a closer acquaintance with you."

She laughed—surprised, relieved, delighted and slightly embarrassed by his show of gallantry. "I think you are too forward, sir," she replied in kind, revealing her eagerness to play this game of turning a new page, to be written on as they pleased.

He gave her a wounded look. "You would forbid me your hand?"

She responded with arch chiding. "If I give you an inch you may take a mile."

He grinned. "And then some."

She shook her head at him. "A dangerous man."

He lowered her hand to cover his heart. "It's true that only the strong dare tread my path with me."

She cocked her head consideringly. "Perhaps a risk must be taken for a gain to be made."

"In meeting a challenge, much can be won," he assured her.

"If you will lead, I *may* follow."

"I trust you are open to persuasion."

Her eyebrows lifted. "That depends on how convincing the persuasion is."

"I shall put my mind to it."

"Your heart, as well, sir, or I shall take my hand back."

He laughed, exhilarated at her matching his flirtatious badinage. But then she always had matched him, before topping the matching with the last word. Not this time, he promised himself. The last word would be his this time.

With slow deliberation he raised her hand to his mouth again, then turned it over and pressed a long, sensuous kiss onto her palm. He saw her eyes widen, heard a gasp escape her lips, and knew the sexual current running through him was just as electric in her.

"Too late. Your hand is mine now," he declared, interlacing his fingers with hers.

She scooped in a quick breath, and with colour high in her cheeks, asked, "Is it safe in your keeping?"

He instantly shot the challenge back at her. "As safe as you want it to be, Samantha."

There was no answer to that. Tommy knew it was

unanswerable because it left the decisions to her. Except he now knew she wanted what he did, knew she actively wanted to satisfy herself with him, and he'd give her every chance, every encouragement, every persuasion to pursue that desire. He was well and truly primed to meet her more than halfway.

Right now, he'd pressed far enough. He lowered her hand, adopting a less aggressively possessive grip to let her feel *safe*, then nodded towards the bridal couple. "I suspect it's time to rejoin the company. The photographer is going into herding mode."

She left her hand in his as he walked her back to the gazebo, a friendly companionable link which his mother immediately noticed.

"Ah, there you are!" she said, satisfaction in her voice and pleasure in her eyes. "I'm just about to collect the children for some photographs by the gate. The pergola and bougainvillea will make a lovely frame."

"Picture perfect," Tommy drawled, referring to the image he was presenting with Samantha, mocking any triumph his mother felt at the current outcome of her interference. What was happening between himself and *the scourge of his life* bore no relation whatsoever to the extracted promise. This wasn't peace. It was war of a different kind...a war shifted onto more delicate ground...an engagement that was very much in the balance, not yet won.

"I think so," his mother returned, unperturbed. "If you'll all go on down...Miranda, Nathan, Jared..." She called them to attention. "...the photographer wants us at the lattice gate."

Jared extracted himself from a group which Tommy recognised as the pearling contingent from Broome. The gap he left revealed a spectacular woman on the other side of it. A mass of black wavy hair sprang away from a centre parting. Her oval face had an exotic cast, almond-shaped eyes, prominent cheekbones, a longish nose, a wide full-lipped mouth. Big jewellery—dangling earrings and heavy necklace in copper, evoking an Aztec design. Her dress shimmered in shades of orange, red, morone, purple—dramatic and daring.

She gave him a curious, assessing look. On some other day he might have followed up that indication of interest, but he had what he wanted right in his hand, and nothing was going to distract him from seeing where it could lead.

"Sam..." Jared spoke her name in that tone of affectionate appreciation that always grated down Tommy's spine, then topped that by spreading his arms wide in a gesture of beholding a vision of beauty. "...you *did* carry it off as superbly as you look."

Tension seethed through Tommy. If Samantha broke free of his handhold and hurtled into his brother's embrace, as she usually did with Jared, he'd pay her back by heading straight for the exotic woman. She'd already snubbed his touch once today, whipping away from it to throw herself into hugging Nathan. All these years, favouring his brothers, throwing them up to him...if she didn't show good faith now, if she was simply testing her desirability out on him...

Her fingers squeezed *his!* Then she turned her gaze up to *him,* sparkling blue eyes inviting more flirtatious fun as she said, "Oh, I just kept telling myself I mustn't fall at Tommy's feet."

"That definitely isn't where I want you," he replied with feeling, delighted when she blushed again, even more delighted with her choice to stay linked to him.

"She was a bundle of nerves before heading up the aisle," Jared explained good-humouredly.

"Then I'm glad I gave her the inspiration she needed to come all the way to me." *All the way,* Tommy vowed to himself, before this day was over. Nothing less would satisfy him.

"Without so much as a tiny falter," Jared added, smiling warmly as he stepped up and curled his hands around her naked shoulders. "A class act, Sam," he purred, and dropped a kiss on her forehead.

The jealousy Tommy had stifled so many times raged through him. "Who's the striking woman in the Broome group?" he sliced at Jared, pointedly training his gaze in her direction.

It served to spring his brother from his familiar fondling. It also caused a flutter in the fingers that had previously squeezed. And so it damned well should, Tommy thought savagely, fed up with watching open affection willingly granted to his brothers. No flinching from their touch! No avoidance of it, either.

"Oh, no you don't!" Jared warned, no purr in his voice now. It was as hard as steel.

Tommy raised his brows in quizzical innocence. "Don't what?"

"Target her," came the sharp retort.

"Now why would I be doing that when Samantha is favouring me with her company?" he asked, flashing her a smile designed to show where his interest lay, while planting a seed of jealousy that would make her work harder at holding his interest. If the interest was genuine and not just a revelling in the power of being a woman who could attract any man. Even Tommy whom she'd snubbed countless times.

This is a two-way street, sweetheart, and don't you forget it! he beamed at her.

"Just let this one go, Tommy. All right?" Jared demanded, completely missing the point.

The dead-serious glint in his younger brother's eyes suggested he was well and truly smitten. "If you're out to impress her, Jared, I'd stop acting so taken by Samantha, if I were you. It gives the wrong signals."

He frowned. "That's easily explained. Sam's part of the family."

"There's no blood relationship between the Kings and the Connellys. Think again, brother."

"Damn it, Tommy! Do me a favour and stick by Sam today. That will sort it out."

"Only if Samantha sticks by me," he countered. "She does have a habit of showing how much she likes you, Jared."

"That's because..." He stopped himself, breath hissing through his teeth as he turned to Samantha. "This is important to me."

"I'll stay with Tommy as long as he stays with me," she assured him, hedging her position.

"Now there's a promise that warms my heart," Tommy rolled out, bitterly resenting the quick understanding between the other two. "And just to show who belongs to whom..." He released Samantha's hand to tuck her arm firmly around his, drawing her into very positive partnership with him. "You can walk on the other side of me, Jared, as we proceed to the gate for more photographs. That should draw the right picture."

They both fell in with this arrangement—no other choice—and Tommy relished the control it gave him. Samantha had come his way and he wasn't about to let her go. If he had to use every tactic he knew, she was going to be his today.

"So who is this new light of your life?" he asked his brother, idly stroking the hand now clinging to his arm. He slid his thumb under her wrist and felt a highly erratic pulse beat, which put a fine zing into his own heated bloodstream.

"You'll meet her in the reception line at the marquee," Jared answered.

Not exactly forthcoming, which piqued Tommy's curiosity. Jared was clearly uncertain of himself with this woman—a tantalising prospect since he readily made multimillion dollar deals in the pearl industry with hard-headed businessmen. Confidence usually oozed from him.

"Give us a name so we don't fumble over it when we do meet her."

"Christabel Valdez."

"Interesting. Where does she hail from?"

An agitated little movement on his arm, fingers curling, nails digging into the fabric of his sleeve. Jealous of his interest? Feeling threatened? How deliciously ironic that she couldn't scorn him for it, not after her promise to Jared.

"Brazil, Holland, Singapore, Australia."

Tommy sifted the information, matching it to the woman and Jared's business interests. "A jewellery designer?"

"Yes. I've just hired her."

"What does Mum think of her work?"

"A risk."

"But you're going to take it."

"Yes."

"Well, good luck to you on both fronts."

It earned a wry smile. "Thanks."

The nails stopped digging. Threat over. But it stuck in Tommy's craw that she thought he would have no conscience about competing against his brothers for a woman either one of them was taken with. To him it was an unbreakable code of honour—respecting each other's territory—no crossing lines drawn unless invited.

He'd known Miranda was Nathan's territory the first night the two of them had met. Not that Nathan had spelled it out as Jared had just done on Christabel Valdez. Nathan wouldn't. But the writing was on the wall the moment he'd offered to show Miranda the Bungle Bungle National Park. She'd gone with Nathan, more or less pressed into the outing, then after that…nothing between them, which had intrigued Tommy into asking her out with him.

Pure curiosity…a little digging in mind…but, of course, Sam had read it differently. As she'd done with the little French piece, Celine Hewson, after he'd fixed things for Nathan and Miranda. No attempt to find out the truth of that tricky encounter or even listen to it. Judged in the worst possible light and slammed for it. Every time.

Until today. And even now the same kind of thinking was undoubtedly simmering away in her mind, ready to leap out and claw him…except it was deeply at odds with the sexual simmering, which he intended to keep fanning to the point where Samantha completely overrode Sam.

The photographer shuffled them around to a pose of his liking, moving Jared to the other side of Nathan and Miranda, with their mother beside him, the children strung out to flank the central group. With Jared out of earshot, Samantha obviously felt driven to comment.

"It's nice that Jared has found someone he fancies, don't you think?"

"Oh, I daresay in his years as a jetsetter he's fancied many women," Tommy responded noncommittally.

"But this one must be special," she pressed, an anxious thread in her voice. "He said she was important to him."

"Well, it's to be hoped she wants what he wants." He slanted a sardonic smile at her. "That's not always the case, is it?"

She looked discomfited. As well she might. Having not wanted what *he* wanted for so many years, she could hardly expect him to put the scars she'd left on him out of his mind and simply take what was now on offer. Though he would take it. If and when she proved she was really serious in wanting him, and not just responding to the excitement of feeling his desire for her.

Her gaze turned back to the milling guests. They had a clear view of Christabel Valdez in profile. Her hair rippled almost to her waist. Some Spanish heritage there, he decided.

"She's very sexy," Samantha murmured.

"Who?"

She frowned at him. "Christabel Valdez."

He pretended to find her. "Do you think so?"

"Don't you?"

"She certainly has the female assets to look desirable, but I've always thought *sexy* was in how a woman responded to me. How she looked at me, acted towards me, and generally showed I was her preferred man."

It startled her into looking back at him.

He smiled, making capital of the eye contact. "I guess what it comes down to is a man wants to be wanted by the woman he wants. Exclusively. Because he's the best man for her. That's what I'd call very, very sexy."

"Yes...exclusively," she repeated, her eyes projecting that very need.

You could have had it anytime. Anytime, he thought, all his most primitive instincts aroused and humming. If you'd ever reached out to me instead of playing your one-upmanship game. If you'd ever paused to ask where I was coming from. Ever tried to understand my needs.

He dropped a kiss on her forehead, wiping out the impression of Jared's mouth on her skin. "For me, you are by far the sexiest woman here today, Samantha," he murmured.

Her breasts heaved delectably under their satin covering. A sigh from her lips feathered his neck. Her eyes sparkled clear happiness.

Which was good.

He didn't want her confused.

He wanted her to give him what he wanted. All of it. And finally concede he *was* the best man, and always would be for her.

CHAPTER SIX

SAM dutifully smiled when the photographer said, "Smile!" but her mind was whirling with what Tommy had told her about showing him he was wanted. She'd never known how to do that. The feminine wiles used by other women had always seemed gross to her. She'd felt she should be valued for her worth as a person, not as a sexpot, trading on all the bits and pieces of her anatomy that could be displayed to provoke lust.

But maybe they were the right signals to excite a man's interest. Maybe she had it all wrong. Or maybe she'd been too frightened of failure to try in case she made a hopeless fool of herself. In moments of sheer desperation she had fantasised playing up to Tommy, but she'd never dared do it until today. Even now she felt self-conscious about it, half expecting him to drop her at the sight of someone more attractive, like Christabel Valdez.

Yet he'd given her every reason to feel positive and confident about what seemed to be happening. Tommy was focusing on her, making her feel sexy and desirable, preferring her over Janice Findlay and every other woman here. All the same, she wished she could feel secure that this was real and not just another playboy game to him.

She thought the desire was real enough. The way

Miranda had dressed her had made her feel different, so she could understand Tommy feeling differently about her, too. But what if it was a novelty that would wear off? What if...

Stop it! Where had negative thinking about Tommy got her? In a pit of her own making! This was her chance to climb out of it. Probably her only chance. She had to risk it. There was no safe course to take. If she ended up hurt, what did it matter? She'd been hurting for years.

"Thank you, children," the photographer said. "You can scoot off. I only want the six adults here now."

For the next ten minutes they were grouped and regrouped in different combinations—the final one being just the three King brothers. Sam couldn't help thinking what handsome men they were as they lined up, chatting and laughing at each other. It seemed odd that neither Nathan nor Jared affected her as Tommy did.

What was it that made Nathan so compellingly special to Miranda? Why didn't Jared set either of their pulses racing? It was only ever Tommy *she* had wanted to impress, Tommy who made her nerves jangle and tied her emotions into painful knots, inevitably plunging her into doing or saying something that put him off instead of drawing him to her.

"Right, gentlemen! Face me and smile," the photographer instructed.

Tommy's gaze zoomed to Sam, and the moment he found hers concentrated on him, the half-smile hovering on his lips widened with a dazzling burst of vitality that zinged straight into her heart, setting off an explosion of joy mingled with a clamouring need for all her fantasies to be answered.

"That's it!" the photographer called when he'd finished clicking.

"I'd like some shots taken of Miranda with me on the western verandah," Nathan requested.

"Lead the way," the photographer agreed affably.

"Sam, will you come with us and make sure I'm arranged right?" Miranda asked.

"I'll come, too. Give you the benefit of my expert eye," Tommy chimed in, waving them both forward. "Clearly I'm the best man to do it."

Miranda laughed and patted him on the cheek as she passed by to join Nathan. "The best, best man. You've been wonderful, Tommy."

"To be faultless is my aim today."

Sam stopped dead, her hopes teetering on the edge of a black abyss. Tommy transferred his devil-may-care grin from Miranda to her and she stared at him, too mortified to take another step. No faults for her to pick on...no baiting...no bickering....

"Is that why you're being nice to me?" she blurted out, unable to bear it if it was.

He frowned, as though not seeing the connection.

"Did Elizabeth ask you to...to make me feel..."

"There you go again!" he broke in, his face tightening in exasperation. "Can you not accept..."

Instant panic. "Yes! Yes, I can!" she cried, frantically denying the negativity. She reached out and grabbed his arm to press her plea. "I'm sorry. I'm just not used to you being..."

"*Nice* to you?" he repeated incredulously. His hand clamped over hers, strong fingers dragging at her skin as though he'd like to dig right inside it. "Believe me! What I'm feeling for you is not an insipid little politeness."

His voice shook with a passion that rocked Sam out of any misconception about his aim where she was concerned.

"Is that how it feels to you...*nice?*" he demanded, his eyes searing hers with their dark blaze.

"Please..." Her chest was so tight she could barely breathe and her heart was thumping like a sledge-hammer. Sheer pressure to come up with something that would blot out her gaffe, stirred her mind into flashing back to the intoxicating fun of their *starting over* repartee. "I want to take this path with you, Tommy, but there are ghosts along it. You said you'd hold my hand."

"Ghosts...ah, yes!" he answered slowly, his mouth curling over the words and his thick lashes half veiling the furnace of feeling in his eyes. "I must admit there are quite a few of those flitting along on both sides of the path. Warding them off does depend on the strength of our togetherness."

He lifted her hand, hooked his arm around hers, then covered her hand again with a reassuring squeeze. "Is that better?"

"Much," she acknowledged in blessed relief.

He swept her up to the homestead verandah, energy pumping from him in such strong waves, it somehow infiltrated Sam's tremulous legs and kept her in pace with him. Her head felt dizzy. She was glad to reach the roofed verandah and get out of the direct heat of the sun.

By the time they walked around to the western side, Nathan and Miranda were already placing themselves in a trial pose for the photographer to find his best angles.

"If you centre them between the verandah posts and feature the frieze above them, it could make a stunning frame," Tommy casually advised.

Sam was amazed he could lift himself so quickly into a natural manner, showing no trace of the contretemps that had almost left her legless. But then he hadn't been at fault. It was she who had come close to shattering the precious peace between them.

Except it wasn't peace.

It was chaos for her.

She felt as though she was skipping from ecstatic elation to despairing torment. Her stomach was a churning mess, her mind a buzz of helpless agitation. It was one thing to fantasise a coming together with Tommy, quite another to experience the reality.

Miranda called her over to make adjustments to the fall of her veil and the drape of her skirt. Tommy stood behind the photographer to get the right view of the pose so he could give her direction on the most artistic arrangement. Working in a harmonious partnership to get the best possible angles and shots soothed some of Sam's inner turmoil. Tommy projected good humour with every bit of helpful advice. An aura of love shone from Miranda and Nathan. Conflict seemed absurd in such a happy atmosphere.

Whenever she stood back to be out of the way of

the photographer, it was obvious why Nathan had chosen this place for the more intimate poses with his bride. It wasn't for the frame of the verandah posts and the ornate frieze that ran around the roof-line of the grand old homestead. It was for the view behind them—the river which was the lifeblood of King's Eden, and beyond it, the vast Mitchell grass plains of the great cattle station stretching to the horizon.

This was Nathan's land, his home, and the heart of the man belonged to it and all it meant to him—his heritage—two million acres of cattle country passing from father to son for five generations—and this was what Miranda had committed herself to sharing with him, all their lives, here in the Kimberly Outback.

Nathan...the firstborn son of Lachlan.

Tommy...the second.

Elizabeth's words suddenly flashed into her mind.... *Tommy's been competing against Nathan all his life. It's why he broke away from Nathan's authority over the cattle station and built up his air charter business.*

Was this wedding conjuring up painful reminders of what could never be for Tommy because he was the second-born son? Was that what he'd meant when he'd referred to ghosts flitting along both sides of the path they were taking today?

Strange, how all these years she'd never really looked at things from Tommy's point of view. She looked at him now, but could not discern any trace of envy in the benevolent smile he was aiming at his brother and his new sister-in-law.

"You're happy for them, aren't you?" she murmured, wanting to tap into the heart he had never shown her.

"Very," he answered warmly, then raised a quizzical eyebrow. "Any reason why I shouldn't be?"

The calmly searching probe of his eyes flustered her for a moment. Was she hopelessly wrong again? "I was wondering if you minded all this...the homestead and station...being passed on to Nathan and Miranda for them to make their lives here."

Not so much as a flicker of reaction. His eyes bored steadily into hers. "As you mind the Connelly station being passed on to your brothers?" he softly answered.

She flushed at the accuracy of that knowledge. "I did at one time," she admitted. "But it doesn't matter now. I've made my own life."

"So have I, Samantha. So have I."

The cold pride on the face he turned away from her made Sam's heart sink. She'd done it again. Struck the wrong chord with him. Better not to try to reach into him. Better to wait until he chose to reveal himself. Which would probably be never if she kept on going like this.

Resolving to keep her mouth firmly shut until he spoke to her, Sam remained doggedly silent while the photography session came to a conclusion.

"I'm going to my room to freshen up before joining the guests again," Miranda announced. "Want to come, Sam?"

Would Tommy wait for her? "No... I...uh, think I'm okay."

"I'll come with you," Nathan said, grinning wickedly at Miranda as he scooped her with him to the door that gave access to one of the hallways of the huge house.

Her husky laugh at his desire to be alone with her brimmed with sexual understanding. Sam stood rooted to the spot, watching them disappear inside, fiercely wishing she could give the same uninhibited response to Tommy, wishing he would just scoop her up and carry her off to his room and...

"Do you envy Miranda?"

She almost jumped at his quiet and all too perceptive question. Heat flared into her cheeks as she tried to banish the wildly carnal thoughts that had sprung into her mind. Agitated that he would be able to read them, she swung her gaze to the photographer who had packed up his gear and was heading down the verandah, back to the main scene of activity.

"I take it your silence means yes. Which leads me to think...you would have liked to marry Nathan yourself."

Shock jolted her into facing him. "That's not true!"

He regarded her with hard scepticism. "You've always looked up to him. As you pointed out to me, he inherits all this, which would undoubtedly have been a feather in your cap since you lose out to your brothers on your own family station. And you *have* displayed considerable feeling for him, Samantha."

"He's always been a friend to me," she expostulated, sickened by the picture Tommy was drawing of her. "But I've never wanted to be his wife. And I've never coveted this place, either. If I envy Miranda, it's because…"

"Because she'll get all his hugs from now on?" His eyes glittered derisively. "Was that your farewell hug to him in the gazebo after the wedding ceremony? Do you feel on the outer now, left without a…"

"Stop it!" She stamped her foot in sheer frustration. "I don't care for Nathan that way."

"Poor Samantha," he drawled. "Do you think I didn't see you sizing the three of us up, out by the pergola? What were you thinking? Nathan married. Jared captivated by Christabel. That only leaves me, doesn't it? Me, whom you've never cared for."

She shook her head, rendered totally speechless by his venomous reading of the situation.

"Well, since you decided to try your womanly wings out on me…" he went on, hooking his arm around her waist and pulling her so hard against him, Sam's hands instinctively flew up to defend herself against his strength, slamming onto his chest.

"…and I disappoint you in every other area…" his voice rolled on, his arm keeping her relentlessly pinned to him as he used his other hand to cup her chin, tilting her face up to his.

Anguished by his angry summation of her attitude to him, Sam didn't know where to begin to refute it. And there was no giving her any time in his eyes. They burned into hers with ruthless intent as he delivered that same intention in speech.

"…I'll try not to disappoint you in the one field where you credit me as an expert. The Playboy King. That's how you refer to me, isn't it?"

Her mouth was too dry to reply.

"But there are always two sides to that game. So why don't you slide those hands up around my neck, Samantha? As you did with Nathan earlier on. As you've done with Jared so many, many times. But never with me."

The seething challenge stirred all the desires Sam had kept hidden. They screamed through her, demanding to have at least this satisfaction. It didn't matter what she said or did, she was never going to win with Tommy, so why not have what she could? He'd invited it, however furiously, and she was not about to deny herself any part of him he offered.

Hands around his neck…

She moved them slowly, her eyes clinging to his with a fierce demand of her own—*don't you dare pull away from me, Tommy King*—as her palms soaked in the strong breadth of his chest, the hard muscle of his shoulders, the tension across his back…and her breasts pressed closer, the stiff, excited peaks of them gradually squashing into the hot wall they met…and she shifted her thighs closer, too, touching, feeling, rubbing as she lifted her arms higher to curl around his neck…every nerve in her body electrically charged with awareness of this man she had wanted for so long, feeding off every bit of contact with him.

His eyes dilated then gathered pinpoints of white-hot light. The vibration of his breathing quickened, the rhythm of it coursing through her sensitised breasts, accelerating her own intake of air. The arm locking her to him shifted, slanting down from her waist, exerting pressure on her lower back, pushing her into a more intimate fit so there was no space at all between them and she could feel the growing hardness of intense arousal—ripples of sweet delight spreading through her from the feeling.

She moved her fingers over his collar, grazing bare skin, gliding up behind his ears, into the thick wealth of springy black curls that matted his scalp. How many times had he ruffled her hair in passing, a tease she'd always hated? But she didn't ruffle his. She luxuriated in the sensual feel of it, softly raking her fingers forward and backward in a slow, loving massage.

His head started bending, eyes coming closer, like black shiny velvet now, and she knew he was about to kiss her and her heart leapt and quivered in almost painful anticipation. It had to be right. It had to be good. It had to be....

His mouth claimed hers in a wild succulent tasting and a terrible greed seized her. She wanted so much, so much, so much...her hands clutching his head, holding it to hers as she responded with a wilder tasting, kisses that taunted his wanting until he proved it with such explosive passion, Sam was lost to the overwhelming excitement of sensations streaming everywhere.

It wasn't just a kiss. It was an invasion of such riveting intimacy, it affected every part of her, arousing a super-sensitivity to the pressure of his body against hers. His hand had left her chin. He held her to him with both arms, and the hard power of his desire was evoking a compelling need in her, an ache, not a sweetness, a fierce ache to have all his mouth promised and more.

"Shall we go to your room?"

His abrupt withdrawal and the hot tingle of his breath on her ear distracted her dazed mind from registering the gruff words. She dragged in a deep breath, wishing he was still kissing her. His mouth was grazing the side of her cheek.

"It's what you want, isn't it?" he murmured.

Yes rushed out of her mind until it belatedly sifted what he'd asked first...*Go to her room?*

Which had to mean...finishing what she'd started in answer to his anger. Her body still screamed *yes*. But reason frantically argued...what about afterwards? How would Tommy feel about her then if he thought she was using him as a Nathan or Jared substitute? It would be awful...awful...

His chest expanded as he lifted his head back from hers, his shoulders squaring. "Shocked to find such strong chemistry between us, Samantha?"

Embarrassed by her own urgent ardour, she slid her hands from his hair, resting them lightly on his shoulders before daring to look up at him. The dark mockery in his eyes sparked a fiery defiance.

"You know how attractive you are to women, Tommy. Why should I be any different?"

"*Nice,* was it?" he bit out.

"Hardly *an insipid little politeness,*" she threw

straight back at him. "More like a volcanic eruption."

"Still quaking?"

"I can feel one section that's rock-hard."

His mouth quirked. "Stimulation tends to do that to a man."

"Well, it *is* nice to know you're not reacting to me as a kid sister anymore."

"Oh, you're definitely all woman today. You now have all the proof you need. Any time you want to take it further..."

Pride instantly whipped out, "I don't really care to join a queue."

"A queue? You?" He threw back his head and laughed.

Sam felt a violent urge to hit him. Wasn't she good enough to line up with the women he'd had in the past? His mouth and body had answered *yes*. If he denied that now she *would* hit him.

The devil was dancing in his eyes when they zeroed in on hers again. "Don't you know you're one of a kind, Samantha Connelly?" He brought up his hand and traced her kiss-sensitised lips with feather-light fingertips as his voice dropped to a low, throaty throb. "Which makes what you just gave me...very special. Uniquely special."

Her heart contracted, then burst into a gallop that flooded wild hope through her veins. She wasn't just another bit of sexual satisfaction...or whatever he got from the women he'd bedded.

"Now come with me," he commanded, turning her to scoop her over to the verandah railing, imprisoning her there, his hands gripping the railing on either side as he stayed close behind, speaking over her shoulder with an intensity that reverberated through her brain. "You see the land out there? It's an elemental part of Nathan. His soul is tied to it. Do you understand what I'm saying?"

"Yes," she whispered, unable to find any volume for her voice, totally confused by his actions and helpless to sort them into a sense she could understand.

"And Jared is fascinated by what can be formed by the forces of earth and nature," he went on. "Gold, diamonds, pearls. Underwater and underground treasures. Remember him panning for gold in the river, back when we were all here together?"

"Yes." The memory was clear, even though nothing else was.

"Finding such things, shaping them into beautiful objects, seeing them enhanced to their most perfect potential...that's in his soul, Samantha. And as lovely as these pearls look on you today, I don't believe they mean anything to you. Do they?"

"Not really," she acknowledged.

"Now look above the land and what do you see?" Nothing but... "Blue sky."

"That's *my* world, Samantha. I don't envy Nathan. I don't envy Jared. Because flying in that sky is what's in my soul. It has no boundaries. It has no substance. But when I'm up there I feel I own it. Or it owns me."

She sighed, realising he was expressing her own

feelings when she was in the air, piloting whatever small craft she'd taken up.

"So where's your soul?" he murmured close to her ear. "Is it bound to the land or flying free up there, Samantha?"

It felt as though he was tugging on her soul...or laying it bare. "Up there," she answered truthfully. There was just no point in lying.

"Then that's something else you share with me...apart from strong chemistry," he said softly. "Or maybe it's part of the chemistry...a soul link like that..."

She felt his lips graze down the curve of her bare neck and shoulder, a trail of warm butterfly kisses that sent little shivers through her heart...almost as though he was caressing her soul, pressing for access. She held her breath in exquisitely tense anticipation of what might come next.

Nothing.

He dropped his imprisoning stance, stepped around her, and turning his back to the view, leaned against the railing, subjecting her to a seemingly objective appraisal from hooded eyes that revealed nothing of his feelings.

"Your lipstick is smudged," he advised her. His mouth curved into a wry little smile. "Best take a visit to your room after all...to freshen up your make-up. There'll probably be more photographs to be taken down by the marquee."

For several wretched moments Sam was ravaged with disappointment. She struggled to interpret what was going on in Tommy's mind. This sexual encounter—if it could be called that—was over. What was she to expect from him now?

"Will you wait here for me?" she asked, feeling he surely must have been establishing further ground for them to tread by suggesting a soul link.

"I've waited a long time for you to join me, Samantha. I'm not about to walk away from finding out what it's worth to me. What's it worth to both of us." He made a casual, invitational gesture. "Something for you to think about, too."

It was certainly that. She *needed* to know its worth more than he could ever guess.

Was he just stringing her along, curious as to which way she'd bounce? It was difficult to know anything with Tommy. He was like quicksilver, impossible to pin down, switching from passionate intensity to blithe spirit in the twinkling of an eye.

"I'll only be a few minutes," she said, and left him, knowing only that he had to spend more hours with her.

Throughout the whole wedding reception they would be seated next to each other at the bridal table in the marquee. Surely in that time she would be able to discern what was serious and what was play in Tommy's behaviour towards her.

A soul link...one of a kind...uniquely special... Sam grasped those words from all he'd said and welded them onto the hope that wouldn't die. They had to mean what she wanted them to mean. *They had to.*

CHAPTER SEVEN

SUNSET was the given time for guests to make their way to the huge marquee which had been set up near the river. It was always a very short twilight in the Kimberly, so even as the sun was sinking below the horizon, turning the river into a gold ribbon and streaking the purpling sky with brilliant colour, the marquee was lit up by thousands of fairy lights, making it look like a magnificent tented palace.

Appreciative remarks flew around the stream of guests walking down the long lawn towards it. Tommy slanted a grin at Sam and remarked, "Trust my mother to come up with the dramatic effect. She's really quite brilliant at organisation."

"It looks very romantic," she replied, unaware of a wistful note creeping into her voice.

"That sounds very much as though you yearn for romance, Samantha. Do you?" he asked, putting her on the spot.

Not playboy stuff, she silently amended, emotionally torn by the charm of manner Tommy had been exerting ever since they'd rejoined the throng of guests. Clearly he had switched into party mode, and while he included her in the smiles and the laughter and the happy banter, he also sought to keep people around them, socialising rather than seeking any further tete-a-tetes with her. It hadn't exactly reinforced the idea she was uniquely special to him.

However, they were more or less in a twosome now, most people focused on heading for the marquee. And he was still holding her hand, though loosely, not possessively.

"I think there's a time and place for romance. Especially when two people love each other," she answered warily.

"And how do you define love?"

The light lilt in his voice turned it into a provocative question rather than a serious one. She decided to toss it back at him.

"How do you define it, Tommy?"

He shrugged. "If I knew, I wouldn't be asking you."

"Well, what do you think it is?" she pressed, secretly glad he hadn't found it with any of the women he'd been involved with.

"I've thought it could be many things, but my feeling now is that it has to be everything. It's been my experience that half-measures never do develop into everything. They just stay…half-measures. And that's not enough."

Sam hadn't expected a serious answer, yet it was one, spoken with a wry self-mockery that underlined disillusionment in the affairs he'd entered into.

"Do I take it Janice was a half-measure?"

"More like a quarter-measure," he answered dryly. "I was feeling low at the time and Janice put a bit of fun into my life for a while."

"Why were you feeling low?"

His eyes glittered briefly at her then looked ahead as he spoke. "Oh, there's this feisty little red-haired witch on my payroll who takes pleasure in cutting me down. Even when I've been acting for the greater good, she never sees it in that light. Just keeps hacking away."

Sam frowned. Was that a fair description of how she treated him? Did she really make him feel *low?*

She flushed as she remembered Elizabeth's words—men wanted to be respected, too. Probably all those women Tommy had been with had respected him and all he stood for, while she...but didn't she deserve respect from him, too?

"It could be a reflex action to the way you treat her," she put forward, trying to keep her voice quiet and reasonable. "Perhaps she feels...down-sized by you."

He threw her a sceptical glance. "Now how could she feel *down-sized* when I trust her to run an important part of my business? And I invariably implement the ideas she comes up with."

He sounded convinced he had always done right by her.

Which bewildered Sam.

Didn't he know it went back long before he'd thought of the wilderness resort, right back to his reaction to her breaking his horse for him, and the way he'd furiously criticised her tactics with the helicopter when they'd been mustering cattle together?

At the time he'd offered her the position of resident pilot for the resort, she'd hoped their relationship would move to a different basis. A more adult basis. Mutual respect. But when she'd asked him why he'd thought of her for the job, what was his answer?

Not, "I want you with me" or "I like having you around" or "I know you'll do it well" or "I trust you more than anyone else."

It was, "You're less likely to kill yourself doing this kind of work."

Maybe he didn't realise what he did to her—all the put-downs that flattened her. In any case, and whatever the truth of his view of their relationship, this was a rare opportunity to reach an understanding with him, and however vulnerable it made her feel, Sam knew she had to seize it. Another time might never come. Besides, it was easier, putting the hostility at a distance, pretending they were speaking of someone else he knew. She chose her words with care, trying to make him see.

"I guess business is one thing and people's personal feelings are another. For example... Do you praise her? Do you make her feel valued? Have you ever shown her approval?"

The ensuing silence gathered a heavy host of memories. Sam swung between surges of guilt and self-justification over her own behaviour, but mostly she felt miserable, wishing their history had been different. She had to concede he had trusted her with a responsible job, and he had taken her ideas on board, but there'd never been any reward for what she'd done. At least, not the reward she'd wanted—having him look at her as he had today, wanting her above every other woman.

"If she feels so ill-used, why hasn't she left and got a position with another charter airline?" came the slightly abrasive reply. "She could have made the competition more competitive."

Sam's heart sank. He saw no blame in himself, or was not prepared to admit to it. In actual fact, she'd thought of leaving him a thousand times. She just couldn't let go.

"If *you* feel so ill-used, why don't you get rid of her?" she countered, her nerves very much on edge now, feeling she had lost and there was nothing she could do about it. How else could she have explained?

It wasn't all her fault, was it?

Panic clutched her again as she looked ahead and saw Elizabeth and Jared already stationed at the entrance to the marquee. There wasn't much time left for private talk. Nathan and Miranda were moving into place, setting up the reception line. She and Tommy would be joining them in a matter of seconds and then they'd be busy, greeting the full complement of guests as they passed by on their way inside.

She couldn't help an anxious glance at him. He caught it and unaccountably, shot her a crooked little smile. Then, as he'd done twice before, he lifted her hand and hooked it around his arm, drawing her into a close togetherness that set her heart fluttering with wild hopes again.

"Why do you suppose neither of us can let each other go, Samantha?" he said softly.

In the twilight his eyes were too dark for her to read, but she felt their intensity, boring into hers,

touching all the raw places he'd opened up. Her mind
burned with the answer... *Because I love you. I've
always loved you. And my life won't be complete
unless you love me right back.* But she couldn't say
those words. They would lay her too unbearably un-
protected if he couldn't return them.

"Something more to think about, isn't it?" he
murmured, then walked her straight to their allotted
position beside the bride and groom.

A stream of guests exchanging a few happy words
with them precluded any thinking beyond meeting
the requirements of being sociable. Most of them
passed quickly by, but Janice's parents, Ron and
Marta Findlay, claimed Tommy's attention for several minutes, waxing lyrical about the wedding and
the setting.

They owned a string of travel agencies across the
Top End—Cairns, Darwin, Wyndham, Kununurra,
Broome—and had been highly promoting Outback
tourism, so they were a good business connection.
Sam wondered how they viewed Tommy's short-
lived affair with their daughter. They showed no sign
of knowing Janice had been comprehensively
dumped. Undoubtedly they would favour Tommy
King as a prospective son-in-law, and they were certainly currying his favour.

Not that they were short of wealth themselves,
Sam thought, eyeing the obviously expensive rings
on Marta Findlay's touchy-feely hand, and her classy
silk dress, featuring a similar deep cleavage to her
daughter's. Nevertheless, if they were into status

symbols, one of the legendary Kings of the Kimberly was probably a prize scalp to bandy around.

Sam felt relieved when Marta unclutched herself from Tommy and moved on with her husband. It was probably foolish to let such women get to her, but they invariably did with their artful little mannerisms, their gushing, their confident awareness of being *female*.

She could feel herself getting prickly every time she met one, and found it extremely vexing that men were suckered in by such stuff. To her mind, it diminished them, which was why she'd been so cutting to Tommy about the women who seemed to fawn over him. Which, according to him, had sent him straight into the arms of Janice Findlay.

Perhaps she was too judgmental. All the same, she had never seen Miranda fawning over Nathan, and they had found what they wanted in each other. Why couldn't it be that way with her and Tommy?

Her parents went by with simply a smile directed at them, not holding up the queue still outside the marquee. Sam reflected her mother had never been a gusher. Nor was Elizabeth King. Though both women had an innate pride in being women. There was definitely something to be learned from them, she decided, wondering if she could reform herself enough to hold Tommy's current interest in her.

"I'm Christabel Valdez," a soft musical voice announced.

Sam, whose gaze had followed her mother, instantly switched it to the woman now standing in front of Tommy, offering her hand.

"We haven't met," she went on.

"No, but Jared has spoken of you," Tommy said warmly, taking her hand as he added, "Welcome to King's Eden, Christabel. I hope you're enjoying yourself."

"Thank you. I now understand why Jared thought a visit here might be inspiring. Your King's Eden has a heart of its own."

She was quite awesomely beautiful, Sam thought—flawless olive skin, magnificent hair and her almond-shaped eyes were not dark as they had looked from a distance—probably the effect of the thick black lashes—but a striking golden amber.

"That it does," Tommy agreed, smiling his most charming smile. "And it tends to call us all back home from time to time."

"Yes," she answered seriously. "I imagine it would do that." She retrieved her hand and gave him a rather formal nod of acknowledgment. "I am pleased to have had the chance to meet you."

"Delighted," Tommy replied, but still she didn't smile at him.

Sam got the strong impression of a very self-contained person who made absolutely no attempt to trade on her spectacular femininity, which in Sam's opinion, left Janice Findlay's for dead. She found herself warmly approving Jared's interest in Christabel Valdez, and she was even more intrigued by her manner as the woman stepped from Tommy to her and offered a smile, as well as her hand.

No smile for Tommy but a smile for her? Sam wondered if Christabel smiled for Jared, or did she keep her distance from all men. It would answer Jared's uncertainty about her response to him.

"Hello," she said far less formally. "Samantha Connelly, is it not?"

"Yes. Nice to meet you, Christabel," Sam returned, giving her hand a friendly squeeze.

Her face lit with warm animation. "May I say I have never seen that lilac colour suit anyone so well. With your blue eyes...I look at you and think of the sky. And that is where you are happy...flying. Yes?"

"Yes." Sam found herself grinning, instinctively responding positively to Christabel Valdez. "There's nothing quite like owning the sky. For me, that is."

"Whereas with me..." she gave a little shrug "...I am suited to the earth colours of Broome. Perhaps I have found my soul-home there."

"Many have. I think more people of different nationalities have settled in Broome than anywhere else. It's like a world of its own. I hope you'll be very happy in your life there."

"Thank you."

With another little nod she moved on. Sam stared after her, suddenly struck by the echo of Tommy's words to her about the sky being in their souls and the earth in Jared's...possibly Christabel's, as well. Had Jared finally found the woman who would share his life?

"What's your impression of her?" Tommy asked between more greetings.

"I liked her. What did you think?" she shot back at him, curious to know his reaction.

"I think Jared will have a tough time winning her."

"Why?"

"She's very guarded."

"She wasn't with me."

He slid her a sardonic look. "You're not a man, Samantha."

It was on the tip of her tongue to remark that *every* woman didn't have to melt at his smile. She barely caught the acid little arrow back. It wasn't a fair comment. And Tommy's was. She'd seen the change in Christabel's manner between Tommy and herself, indicating the relaxing of a guard she kept with men that she didn't find necessary with women.

Sam wondered what had happened in her life to make her like that. It wasn't really fair to keep all men at bay on the basis of past experiences. Nevertheless, wasn't she herself doing a similarly unfair thing to Tommy, all too ready to snipe at him even when he was being reasonable? If she didn't stop it, she'd drive him away again. After all, why should he take nasty barbs from her when there were so many women who'd be sweet to him?

Here she was, standing shoulder to shoulder with him, sharing a togetherness she wanted, knowing that despite everything that had gone on between them, he wasn't about to let her go. If she hung on to him and kept being a desirable woman instead of a witch, she might be a winner instead of a loser.

Sam had no sooner thought this than her stomach curdled at the sight of her brother, Greg, with Janice Findlay hanging all over him, clutching his arm, squashing her ample cleavage around it as she poured sweet sexy suggestiveness into his ear. Sam just knew it had to be sexy because Greg's face was flushed, his eyes bright with excitement, and Janice had a feline smugness written all over her face. She was creaming him and Sam hated it, certain it was a tit for tat for Tommy's defection, which meant her brother was being taken for a ride.

"Well, Sam-m-m..." she purred, completely ignoring Tommy. "I didn't know you had such a hunky brother. I do so lu-u-u-v men of the land." She accompanied this with a fingernail stroke down this chest, bisecting the space between the lapels of his suit.

Greg laughed with a kind of embarrassed pleasure. His first hot come-on, Sam thought caustically.

"Greg is a great guy, Janice. Maybe you should take the time to get really acquainted with him."

"Oh, I intend to. There's something about weddings that makes one feel..." She let the word linger, sliding a catty look at Tommy, then back at Sam. "...deliciously horny."

With a provocative little laugh, Janice snuggled up to Greg again and carried him off into the marquee.

Before she could stop herself, Sam threw a dagger-like look at Tommy. "And *that* kind of mush from Janice made you high again?"

His eyes hardened into smoking black coals. "Don't knock it, Samantha. There are times when a man simply wants to feel wanted. As Greg does right now."

She flushed and dropped her gaze, painfully aware she hadn't made Tommy feel wanted. Until today.

"And she's probably right about weddings," he drawled sardonically. "Seems to me you were very definitely turned on when you kissed me on the verandah."

That was different. Entirely different. "She's using Greg as a substitute. You know she is, Tommy," she said fiercely.

"And you weren't?"

"No!" she flared at him. "I wanted…"

"Me?" His eyes glittered at her, pinning her down.

There was nowhere to go but the truth. "Yes. I wanted to know what it might be like with you."

"And I, with you, Samantha," he returned, giving her the instant relief of knowing he wasn't about to use her admission to any mean advantage. "Do you have a mind to continue this journey of discovery with me?"

"Yes," she said recklessly.

"Good! Because that's what I'd like, too."

A dizzy sense of triumph fuzzed her mind. Everything she'd risked so far had paid off. Tommy *was* reviewing their relationship, wanting more from it, wanting to see where it might lead if they gave it a chance to move forward.

It didn't occur to her until they were on their way into the marquee that the questions he'd put to her were all related to "feeling horny."

Had she just committed herself to having sex with him?

Did he have anything more than that in mind?

Her heart started fluttering.

Then a fierce resolution kicked in.

I don't care. I'll have whatever I can have of Tommy King. At least then I'll know how much I mean to him.

CHAPTER EIGHT

ELIZABETH smiled as she watched Nathan and Miranda happily positioning themselves for the cake-cutting ceremony. What was it...ten months since she had interviewed Miranda for the position of resort manager? Something about her had stirred the hope she might be the right one for Nathan, the one to draw him out of his entrenched view that no woman could be kept happy with his kind of life.

Here they were...married...and Elizabeth had no doubt the marriage would last. The love and need they had for each other carried the same strength she knew were in their characters. They would stand together through any adversity, those two, and it gave her a deep sense of satisfaction that she had selected Miranda for King's Eden.

There would be children now...the next generation. Lachlan would have wanted the family line to go on. At least one decisive step in that direction had now been taken, but one wasn't enough. Who could read the future? Never, for one moment, had she imagined Lachlan's life being cut short...her indomitable husband...gone...and all she had left of him were their three sons.

It wasn't enough.

She wanted to see Lachlan in the children of their children. She wouldn't let it end. And while Nathan was most like his father, that was no guarantee his children would get the major share of Lachlan's genes. It could be Tommy's children, or Jared's who inherited them. Life was a lottery, no guarantees, and the best chances had to be taken, not wasted.

The five-piece band she'd hired struck up a fanfare as the cake was finally cut. A loud round of applause followed, then the announcement from the master of ceremonies, ''The new Mr. and Mrs. King will now proceed to the dance floor for the bridal waltz.''

''Ready to follow them on and show them how to waltz, Mum?'' Jared teased, rising from the chair beside her.

She smiled at her youngest son as he assisted her onto her feet. In some ways she was closest to Jared who had taken on and expanded the business she'd inherited from her father. He had an intuitive understanding of her interest in the pearl industry, and God knew she'd needed some interest to focus on after Lachlan had died.

''You know,'' Jared murmured, having taken her arm for the walk to the dance floor, ''Tommy and Sam seem to be getting it together for once. Not one spat that I've seen. And looking at them now, getting up to dance...''

She looked. They were sparkling at each other and the electric charge running between them was definitely positive, their body language emitting an eagerness to dance together—anticipating pleasure, no mere sufferance for the sake of good form. For the truce she had asked for to have lasted this long—

close to six hours now—was a major miracle, and Elizabeth prayed they had settled their differences.

"It's about time they got it together," she murmured to Jared. "All these years of mutual frustration…"

"Well, Sam's sure got him snagged today," he returned laughingly. "Miranda made a great choice with that bridesmaid outfit."

"I hope Tommy is seeing further than that."

And she'd make it her business to ascertain what was actually going on there. There would be a rotation of partners during the bridal waltz. It would probably be her only chance this evening to get Tommy to herself for some straight talking.

The band started up, swinging into a waltz number, and Nathan and Miranda circled the floor, transmitting the magic of their wedding to everyone watching. Jared timed their entry with smooth grace, and Tommy whirled Samantha onto the floor with his usual zestful panache. Samantha's face was lit with happy excitement. It gave Elizabeth's heart a lift. True happiness…so hard to come by at times.

She glanced up at Jared and found his gaze trained on the table where Christabel Valdez sat. He was very taken by her. She was certainly a highly creative, innovative designer, but Elizabeth felt uneasy about a relationship developing between the beautiful Brazilian and her youngest son.

Behind the practised serenity of those golden-amber eyes, Elizabeth sensed many secrets which Christabel didn't care to bring into the light of day. Widowed, she'd said, perhaps giving legitimacy to the child she had, a little girl Jared had met by accident, not by active introduction.

And why did she continue to live in the caravan at the Town Beach in Broome, despite her current, very well-paid employment? It smacked of a deliberate choice to maintain a temporary place rather than get into a fixed address. Elizabeth didn't have the answers and the younger woman never invited any intrusion into her private life.

Christabel…she had an exotic quality that appealed to Jared. Elizabeth understood the attraction but it was worrying. She didn't want to see her youngest son hurt by it. Still, there was nothing she could do to avert that outcome. Some things just had to run their course.

"On to Nathan, Mum," Jared warned, giving her a whirl towards her eldest son before turning to take Samantha as his partner.

Nathan smiled at her as he took her in his arms. "You've done a wonderful job with the wedding, Mum. It's everything I wanted for Miranda. And your speech, welcoming her into the family…" His smile turned crooked. "…it meant so much, she was moved to tears."

"She *is* everything I wanted for you in a wife, Nathan."

He sighed contentedly. "Me, too. Lucky you hired her to manage Tommy's resort, wasn't it?"

"Yes. Though I recall you weren't too pleased with my choice of a woman manager at the time," she archly reminded him.

He laughed. "I changed my opinion the moment Miranda walked into my life."

"So you revealed in your speech." She smiled, enjoying her own secret triumph over bringing them together. "It was a lovely speech, Nathan. It moved *me* to tears."

"Just as well Tommy got us all laughing when he got up to do his best man bit. He really is a brilliant raconteur. Had everyone hanging on his next line."

"It was certainly a good performance," she agreed. The question was whether it was also a performance with Samantha. Tommy was very very good at putting on a show.

"I thought what he said about Sam was nice, too," Nathan warmly added. "Did you see her glow when he praised her for being the best helpmate anyone could ask for?"

"Yes. I'm glad he was kind."

"Mmmh…" His vivid blue eyes twinkled. "Might be a bit more than kindness, Mum. You can check him out on that one. It's his turn to dance with you."

He passed her on to Tommy who put his own unique style to the waltz steps, grinning as she matched his timing. "At last…the perfect partner!"

She raised her eyebrows. "I think someone younger should fill that position for you."

He laughed, exuberant with the excess energy that always marked high spirits in Tommy. "And very shortly will. The force is with me tonight."

"What force is that?"

Wicked teasing in his eyes. "The force that turns a witch into a princess."

Samantha! But how serious was he about claiming her as his perfect partner?

"Does this force last beyond the spell of the wedding?" she asked, keeping her voice tuned to light banter.

"Who knows? Will the prince turn back into a frog?"

"I've always thought faith could work miracles."

"Only if it's strong enough and never wavers."

"You've never been weak, Tommy. You can make it strong if you want to."

"If the ghosts stay away. Many ghosts, Mother dear. Many, many ghosts."

Yes, she thought. They'd both inflicted scars that weren't easy to push into the past.

"Take care, Tommy."

His eyes glittered down at her. "No. Taking care is not what tonight is about. What's the old saying...there's a tide in the affairs of men? Tonight I ride it. I ride it for all it's worth. And if it tosses me up on a desolate island...then it's done, isn't it?"

Such fierce, reckless passion...it was in his eyes, in his voice, in his words. All or nothing. Pride. That had always been the devil in him.

"You are now invited to join the King family on the dance floor," the master of ceremonies announced.

"Back to Jared," Tommy lilted, and passed her on to his younger brother before Elizabeth could think of anything to say that might temper the course he was bent on taking.

She looked back.

He was masterfully gathering Samantha into a dance hold that pressed every intimacy that had once banned the waltz from respectable gatherings. And the princess went willingly.

Elizabeth knew in that moment there *was* nothing she could do or say to change anything.

Good or bad…they held their own destiny in their hands.

CHAPTER NINE

FOR SAM, it was definitely the best evening of her life. She'd been the main focus of Tommy's attention ever since they'd entered the marquee—warm, considerate, charming, flattering attention—with only the occasional teasing remark. But it wasn't put-down teasing, more wickedly sexy, sparking a wonderfully intimate sense of fun that was more intoxicating than the champagne they drank.

And dancing with him was more thrilling than she'd ever imagined. All these years, whenever she'd seen him dance with other women, envy had been like a knife in the heart. Quite simply, he was the best, so attuned to rhythm he could create his own version of steps, adding an exciting challenge to the sheer pleasure of moving with him.

Often she'd meanly called him a flashy show-off, though she knew it was only because he didn't ask her to partner him. There wasn't a woman alive who wouldn't love to dance with Tommy King. He made the music come alive so physically, it was as though her whole body, and his, were instruments, too, pulsing to the beat, expressing the melody, making it mean more than it ever had before.

Best of all, was the sense of being one with him, and not just in moving around the dance floor. It was marvellous not to feel inhibited by the close body

contact, to revel in Tommy's strong masculinity
without any fear of his pulling away or rejecting her
for some other more desirable woman. For tonight,
at least, he was willingly, happily hers.

As the evening wore on, the band wound up, rolling out great sets of rock numbers from each de-
cade—Bill Haley, Elvis, the Beatles, Abba, Neil
Diamond, Michael Jackson. Everyone was singing
and clapping. The men discarded jackets and ties as
the party really began to swing.

At first, Tommy was fairly conservative in throwing himself into the jazzier numbers, waiting to see
if Sam was comfortable with where he led. When
she easily matched him and started throwing in a few
little innovative movements of her own, he laughed
and moved into top gear, challenging her in an exhilarating mutual contest that ended up with the rest
of the dancers standing back to watch and clap and
urge them on to wilder feats.

Sam was barely aware of them. She was totally
captivated by the sexual energy pouring from
Tommy, the sense of being stalked, tantalised, his
dark eyes wickedly telling her he could take her
whenever he wanted, but not yet…not yet because
he wanted to revel in every anticipatory move,
wanted to watch her responding to him, wanted to
build the excitement, to savour it, to exult in it.

And she was possessed by the same energy, her
heart pumping a wild pagan beat, her body moving
with provocative intent, her arms beckoning, retreat-
ing, pretending an aloof self-containment while her

eyes flirted with the burning purpose in his, and her feet glided and stamped and twirled.

Finally he pounced, trapping her legs between his, bending her over his arm in a deep swoop. His face hovered above hers, a triumphant grin on his face. Then while she was helpless to prevent it, he snatched the lilac rose from her hair with his teeth. As the band brought the number to a loud drumming end, echoing the mad drumming of her heart, Tommy lifted her upright again, stepped back to sketch a gallant bow, and presented her with the rose in a chivalrous gesture of homage, to huge applause and cheers from the onlookers.

"Champagne for my lady?" Tommy twinkled at her, sweeping her off the dance floor towards the bar which had been set up near the exit from the marquee.

Sam nodded, laughing breathlessly, still exhilarated and loving him for the very playboy qualities she had told herself she despised. Which had never been true. She knew that now. It had simply been a case of wanting him to play with her.

The barman poured their drinks. Tommy clicked his glass against hers. "To the perfect partner," he murmured, his eyes still hot from the mating ritual they'd so blatantly started.

"For me, too," she answered huskily, bubbling with an excitement that had more to do with the champagne of this night with Tommy than with the bubbly liquid she sipped.

"I didn't know you could dance like that,

Samantha,'' he commented quizzically. "You never have at the few parties we've both attended.''

"There aren't many men who can dance like you,'' she answered, stating the honest truth. Then with a little shrug, denying it mattered right now, she added, ''And you chose other women to partner you.''

His mouth curled with irony. "I did ask you once. You told me you didn't care to make an exhibition of yourself.''

She flushed, vividly remembering that one wretched occasion. It was the opening of the wilderness resort party, and Tommy had been high on the successful completion of his dream tourist venture, his exuberant spirits bursting to be expressed. He'd grabbed her hand, arrogantly commanding as he said, ''Come on, Sam. Let's pound the floor. Show 'em how fantastic we feel about this.''

And she'd baulked, knowing how inept she would be in matching him, lacking the confidence to try, afraid of looking awkward and foolish, spoiling his desire to express all she didn't know how to express.

"I couldn't do it then, Tommy,'' she confessed, grimacing at the memory of how she'd refused him, her wayward tongue tripping out that harsh defence. ''I'm not a natural like you,'' she explained. "I had to learn.''

"Learn?'' he repeated, frowning at what was obviously an alien idea to him.

She nodded. "When the Big Wet came that year, I went to Darwin and took a course of dance lessons.

All the modern stuff. Jazz ballet. I had to learn to loosen up, go with the flow.''

He shook his head in bemusement. ''You could have asked me to teach you.''

She returned his ironic smile. ''I thought you'd make fun of me. Or get impatient, exasperated...''

''No,'' he cut in, his face tightening, his eyes glittering with bitter accusation. ''You couldn't bear not being competitive. That's the truth of it, isn't it?''

Her heart stopped, and all the pumped-up excitement drained away. ''Maybe it was,'' she admitted flatly. ''I don't know anymore. All I know is...you never asked me to dance with you again...until tonight...and I wasn't competing with you just now. I was...''

Despair clutched her mind. Would they never understand each other? Always be ships passing on contrary courses? Her eyes pleaded against the harsh judgment in his and she heard her voice wobbling as she begged his understanding.

''This probably sounds crazy...but I wanted to...to share things with you...to be able to do what you could...and...and have you feel proud of me.''

Tears blurred her eyes. She fumbled the glass down on the bar table. ''Excuse me,'' she gabbled, and virtually blundered her way outside, her heart aching with the burden of always getting it wrong, somehow destroying the very thing she most wanted. And it *was* her fault. She had said those miserable things to Tommy, casting him in a lesser light because of her own sense of inadequacy, of never seeming to measure up in his eyes.

PLAY THE
Lucky Key Game
and get

HOW TO PLAY:

1. With a coin, carefully scratch off gold area at the right. Then check the claim chart to see what we have for you — **2 FREE BOOKS** and a **FREE GIFT** — **ALL YOURS FREE!**

2. Send back the card and you'll receive two brand-new Harlequin Presents® novels. These books have a cover price of $3.99 each in the U.S. and $4.50 each in Canada, but they are yours to keep absolutely free.

3. There's no catch. You're under no obligation to buy anything. We charge nothing —ZERO — for your first shipment. And you don't have to make any minimum number of purchases — not even one!

4. The fact is, thousands of readers enjoy receiving books by mail from the Harlequin Reader Service®. They enjoy the convenience of home delivery...they like getting the best new novels at discount prices, BEFORE they're available in stores...and they love their *Heart to Heart* subscriber newsletter featuring author news, horoscopes, recipes, book reviews and much more!

5. We hope that after receiving your free books you'll want to remain a subscriber. But the choice is yours — to continue or cancel, any time at all! So why not take us up on our invitation, with no risk of any kind. You'll be glad you did!

YOURS FREE!
A SURPRISE MYSTERY GIFT

We can't tell you what it is...but we're sure you'll like it! A
FREE GIFT–
just for playing the
LUCKY KEY game!

Visit us online at
www.eHarlequin.com

FREE GIFTS!

NO COST! NO OBLIGATION TO BUY!
NO PURCHASE NECESSARY!

PLAY THE
Lucky Key Game

Scratch gold area with a coin.
Then check below to see the gifts you get!

YES! I have scratched off the gold area. Please send me the 2 Free books and gift for which I qualify. I understand I am under no obligation to purchase any books, as explained on the back and on the opposite page.

NAME   (PLEASE PRINT CLEARLY)

ADDRESS

APT.#   CITY

STATE/PROV.   ZIP/POSTAL CODE

🔑🔑🔑🔑 **2 free books plus a mystery gift**	🔑🔑🔑 **1 free book**
🔑🔑🔑 **2 free books**	🔑🔑 **Try Again!**

Offer limited to one per household and not valid to current Harlequin Presents® subscribers. All orders subject to approval.

(H-P-OS-07/00)

The Harlequin Reader Service® — Here's how it works:

Accepting your 2 free books and gift places you under no obligation to buy anything. You may keep the books and gift and return the shipping statement marked "cancel." If you do not cancel, about a month later we'll send you 6 additional novels and bill you just $3.34 each in the U.S., or $3.74 each in Canada, plus 25¢ delivery per book and applicable taxes if any.* That's the complete price and — compared to cover prices of $3.99 each in the U.S. and $4.50 each in Canada — it's quite a bargain! You may cancel at any time, but if you choose to continue, every month we'll send you 6 more books, which you may either purchase at the discount price or return to us and cancel your subscription.

*Terms and prices subject to change without notice. Sales tax applicable in N.Y. Canadian residents will be charged applicable provincial taxes and GST.

If offer card is missing write to: Harlequin Reader Service, 3010 Walden Ave., P.O. Box 1867, Buffalo NY 14240-1867

BUSINESS REPLY MAIL
FIRST-CLASS MAIL   PERMIT NO. 717   BUFFALO, NY

POSTAGE WILL BE PAID BY ADDRESSEE

HARLEQUIN READER SERVICE
3010 WALDEN AVE
PO BOX 1867
BUFFALO NY 14240-9952

NO POSTAGE
NECESSARY
IF MAILED
IN THE
UNITED STATES

Tears of hopelessness trickled down her cheeks. She turned up towards the house, forcing her tremulous legs into the necessary action to get her to a safe refuge. Impossible to face anyone right now. Her mascara was probably running. Best to pin the stupid rose back in her hair and armour herself again to see the wedding reception through as a good bridesmaid should.

She was never going to make it with Tommy. All this evening…just a fool's paradise…a bubble of fragile happiness too easily broken. Underneath the charm she'd been basking in, Tommy had such a deep store of anger against her, and rightly so. She'd never done anything to make him feel good about himself, tearing strips off him, shunning him in favour of his brothers…the sins were endless.

How could he forget them?

She kept trudging up the long lawn, dying a little with every step, knowing she couldn't turn back the clock, wishing Tommy would come after her, accepting there was no real chance with him anyway.

Vulnerable! Tommy stood in a shocked daze as that word—his mother's word for Samantha—drummed through his mind. He hadn't believed it. He'd scorned the very idea of Samantha Connelly having any soft underbelly to be ripped open…revealing such naked hurting.

He'd been wrong.

All these years he'd been wrong.

She'd been fighting to win his admiration, wanting approval, appreciation, and he'd seen it as—he shook his head—everything else but that...turning to other women to get what she didn't give...only it was never enough because he wanted it from her.

Hell hath no fury like a woman scorned... The jibes about his affairs...they were understandable if she wanted him and thought he didn't see her as good enough. Had she wanted him all along? Had they both trodden a path of misconceptions about each other?

Her eyes filling up with tears...

She'd never cried...too strong, too proud, too gritty to show any womanly weakness. But today had been different. Tonight had been different. And be damned if he was going to lose that difference now!

Gripped by the need to act, Tommy set his glass on the bar table and headed straight for the exit, determined on following Samantha, catching her, straightening things out between them. He was waylaid, his arm clutched, with a drunken Janice Findlay swinging on it, lurching around to face him and grab a handful of his shirt.

"Hold it, lover!" she slurred, leering at him as she added, "You and I need to talk."

"Not now!" he clipped out, trying to pluck her hand away without offensive force.

She dug her nails into the fabric and snarled, "Don't think you can throw me off, Tommy King."

She was dangerously drunk, he belatedly recognised, and cast a quick glance around for Greg, hoping for handy assistance in disentangling himself.

"Hot to hump Sam Connelly, aren't you?" Janice

taunted. "But she's given you the slip and I've got you. Been waiting all night for this."

No Greg in sight, but he caught Jared's eye and aimed a frown towards Janice, indicating a problem. Taking a deep breath and telling himself to calm his sense of urgency, he met his ex-playmate's venom with as much reasonableness as he could muster.

Stroking the grasping hand to relax the grip she had on him, he spoke in a gentler tone. "What is it you want, Janice? You know it's over between us. Holding me like this won't lead anywhere. What more is there to say?"

"Think you can get off scot-free, don't you?" she jeered. "One of the great Kings of the Kimberly." She released his shirt to throw off the touch of his hand in a gesture of contempt. "You're going to pay for the pleasure you took with me. I'll make your name dirt if you don't."

"I hope you'll think better of that in the morning, Janice. In the meantime..."

"Ah, there you are..." Jared smoothly scooped her aside, a strong, purposeful arm around her waist. "...Greg was worried you might get lost going to the loo. I said Christabel would accompany you, make sure..."

Tommy didn't hear the rest. He was out of the marquee and moving fast, head swivelling, looking for a lilac gleam to follow. No sight of anything likely along the riverbank. How big a start did Samantha have? What with sorting himself out and Janice delaying him, several minutes must have passed.

His heart kicked into a greater sense of urgency as he scanned the lawn leading up to the house. There, close to the bougainvillea hedge... He broke into a run, uncaring what anyone who saw him thought. It might be his life on the line here—as good as—if what he'd worked out was right.

She was heading for the front gate, in the dark shadows thrown by the trees beside the circular driveway. Was it her? Instinct insisted it had to be. His feet pounded over the grass. She obviously couldn't hear him coming. There was no pausing from her, no turning around. Was he pursuing a ghost?

Struck by an uncharacteristic stab of anxiety, he called out, "Wait!"

Tommy's voice? Sam's heart contracted. She looked back towards the marquee. A black and white figure was pelting up the lawn, making a beeline to where she was. It had to be Tommy...having decided he should fetch her back no matter what, mend the ruction, see the night through, hold the happy family line, the dutiful best man.

Sam instantly put on a spurt, past the lattice gate, running up the path, the steps onto the verandah, panicking at the thought of facing anything with Tommy right now. It wouldn't be about caring what she felt. He would have followed her sooner if he'd really cared about her. As for the sexual thing that had been zipping between them...it was just Tommy being the way he was with other women...nothing special to her, except perhaps an extra zing of titillating interest because it was out of their usual pattern.

She rushed into the house, along the halls to her room, needing to shut Tommy out, to give herself time to get this nerve-shuddering misery under control and paste over the cracks...make-up, hair, heart. A half hour break. Excuses could easily be made to cover that.

Tommy couldn't be sure who it had been out there. She hadn't answered him and the darkness would have precluded positive identification. Hopefully he would think he'd made a mistake, wander back and get involved with other company. Then she could turn up in the marquee again and pretend nothing was amiss.

She whirled into her room, closing the door as fast as she could. Safe, she thought, and without switching on the light, tottered over to the bed and sat down to catch her breath. The ache inside her hurt so much she sagged forward, elbows on knees, head in her hands. Somehow she had to hold herself together, finish the night.

Tomorrow she would fly home with her parents and brothers. The resort had closed, the tourist season over for the year. Tommy didn't need her, not in any sense. He could manage without her services as a pilot in his KingAir charter business. She needed time away from him, away from anything to do with him. Best to go home, lick her wounds, get herself into shape to face a different future from the one she had no hope of having.

Her heart jumped as she heard footsteps thumping

along the hall. Before she had time to think, her door crashed open and the room was flooded with light. Tommy stood there, his hand still on the light-switch, his chest heaving, his face strained, his dark eyes wildly targeting her, and tension flooded from him, swirling around her, stiffening her spine and pulling her onto her feet in a fierce burst of outrage at his intrusion.

"This is my *private* room! You have no right to..."

"As I see it, we've kept too much private from each other," he sliced in, vehemently denying her protest and closing the door, punctuating his determination to confront no matter how she felt about it.

"I'm sick of arguing with you!" she cried, her hands curling into fists.

"So am I," he retorted.

"Then what are you doing here?" She barely repressed the urge to fly at him and fight him out of her room.

"I'm here because I want you. What's gone on between us in the past doesn't matter a damn! I want you, Samantha Connelly..."

The passion in his voice brought the raging turbulence inside Sam to a paralysing stop. Her mind was only capable of clutching and repeating one thought. *He meant it....he meant it...*

"...and I think you want me!"

CHAPTER TEN

SAM STARED at Tommy, all her yearning for him mixed with the panicky doubt that this might not be the real thing. His desire for her right now was real. It was burning in his eyes, making her churn with the treacherous excitement that had gripped her earlier this evening. Except she knew now that just having sex with him wouldn't be enough. She wanted it all...what Miranda had with Nathan...and if Tommy was only wanting to be satisfied on some libido level...

He took a step towards her, emanating unshakable purpose. It propelled Sam into dashing away from the bed, frantically, instinctively, needing time and space to sort out what was happening. She caught sight of herself in the dressing-table mirror and jerked to a halt, momentarily mesmerised by the reflection of a stranger to her real self—huge eyes smudged with make-up she never normally used, skin unmarred by freckles, sophisticated hairstyle, expensive jewellery, sexy dress.

"It's not me!" The words burst out of her painful confusion and gathered a hysterical momentum. She swung to face Tommy, to confront him with the *real* truth. "You never wanted me before. It's this..." She lifted her hands and flung them down in a fierce dismissal of how she looked today. "...this get-up!" she finished contemptuously.

"I did want you," he declared without batting an eye. "I always wanted you."

Oh, no! She shook her head at such a terrible lie. She didn't believe it. Couldn't believe it.

He took another step towards her. Another step.

"Stop it, Tommy!" she commanded, her voice shaking in violent protest. She knew there was a box of tissues on the dressing-table. Blindly grabbing, she pulled out a bunch of them and wiped them over her painted face, savagely destroying the work of the beautician. "See? This is me!" she hurled at him. "The Sam who isn't worth a second look from you."

He kept coming at her.

She dropped the tissues and attacked the pins holding up her hair, tearing them out, throwing them away, messing up the artificial sophistication. "You never wanted this, and this is who I am...the carrot mop-top...not to be taken seriously as a woman...the pesky squirt in the background...the freckle-faced..."

He caught her wrists and dragged her hands down, forcing them to rest against his chest, holding them there. "The feisty, freckle-faced girl I wanted to impress but never seemed able to," he said, his voice like a burr in her ears, determinedly penetrating the chaos running through her.

"The fellow spirit who feels as alive in the sky as I do," he went on, the words making her temples throb. "The woman whose beautiful, burnished curls are like magnets to my fingers...and my need to touch them could only be covered by a teasing manner because I believed you didn't want to be touched by me.''

His chest expanded as he inhaled a deep breath, and his eyes seared hers of any further covering up by either of them. ''But that's not true, is it, Samantha?''

She crumpled, unable to hold up the shields she'd hidden her feelings behind for so long. ''I didn't mean to drive you away from me, Tommy. I didn't mean to...to...'' Her lips trembled. Her throat choked up. She could feel his heart thumping under her palm. Were they touching now? Was this the truth?

''Tell me you want me,'' he demanded hoarsely.

Her truth spilled out, heedlessly, compulsively, irrevocably. ''I want you.''

For a long nerve-tearing moment, their eyes locked, a fierce, primitive challenge surging between them—no holds barred—the final ripping away of years of destructive pretence and the passion for proof of the desire declared was a violent force, climbing, clawing its way past the old inhibitors, scattering the ghosts, screaming to be satisfied to the very core of absolute truth.

Then his mouth crashed onto hers, explosively invasive, demanding a response to match his driving need, and Sam poured all her craving for him right back, voraciously and exultantly feeding the deep wrenching hunger for the feel of him, the taste of him, the heart, the mind, the soul of him.

He kissed her with the same ravening appetite,

binding her to him with an ardour that drew on everything she was, and the rush to give—to give and take—was a raging wanton wildfire, racing through her entire body. This time he was hers. Absolutely hers. His mouth, his hands, the hard, hot yearning of his body were telling her so.

Fingers kneading her hair, kisses adoring her face, burning down her throat, heating her bare shoulders; her own hands revelling in the ripple of muscles on his back, her breasts peaking with almost painful excitement, her stomach and thighs quivering with pleasure under the strong, masculine pressure he exerted on them, all her senses swimming in the intoxicating delight of his desire for her.

The zipper at the back of her dress fell open, loosening the boned bodice, the tight fit around her waist and hips. Tommy lifted her up, hauling her out of the satin sheath, burying his face between her breasts as though inhaling the scent of her and savouring the softness of her flesh as he carried her over to the bed and laid her on the quilt.

His eyes glittered over her. "Look at you," he said with an intense mixture of admiration and awe.

And she realised he loved the look of her and a glorious swell of pride swallowed up any chilling nervousness about her nakedness.

He threw off her shoes, peeled down her pantihose. "Silky red curls. I knew there would be," he murmured gruffly, tossing the last garment aside and thrusting his hand through the curls, reaching into the apex of her thighs, stroking, inflaming a tumult of sensation as he bent over and kissed her breasts, leaving them throbbing with his need to possess, aching to be taken like that again and again.

"Don't move," he muttered fiercely as he drew back. "I've never seen you like this and I've wanted to...all these years...you naked on a bed, open to me, wanting me to come to you."

The heat of his words consumed any inhibitions she might have had as she lay there, her pulse racing, her stomach churning with fever-pitch anticipation as she watched him discard his clothes. Her eyes gloated over the smooth sheen of his tanned skin, the nest of black curls across his chest, arrowing down to the flat tautness of his stomach. Her heart kicked at the sheer power of his aroused sexuality. This was Tommy wanting her...the only man in her life she had ever wanted...and excitement writhed through her. Her arms lifted, welcoming, yearning, dying to hold him to her, feel him, love him.

"Samantha..." It was a low, animal growl, a deep affirmation of who and what she was to him as he came to her, gathering her to him, flesh to flesh, a glorious pagan freedom in their touching, their kissing, the feverish need to savour every inch of each other, to drown in the sheer sensuality of this magical experience, to capture every drop of knowledge to be treasured...this first time, the reality of a dream coming true...and it was wonderful, incredibly satisfying, beyond any imaginable feelings.

Tommy...her King...and when finally, frantically, she arched herself to take him inside her, urging the ultimate intimacy, the wild, tremulous anticipation that seized her was ecstatically answered. He *was* the king of all men, the fullness of his power driving forward, possessing the path she'd most wanted him to take, the path that fused them together, and from it radiated a pulsing energy so intense, Sam was lost in a chaotic internal world, a place that shimmered to the beat of his will to be one with her, onwards, inwards, a deep rhythmic giving of himself, and she receiving the bliss of it, winding herself around him, holding on to the riveting sensation of travelling with him, the blind ecstasy of feeling him taking her further and further towards some sweet pinnacle of perfection.

It burst upon her in convulsive waves, his release, her release, great molten spasms of pleasure, and she clutched him to her, hugging the sense of absolute togetherness, wanting to feel totally immersed in his life-force, belonging to him and with him. His arms burrowed under her, hugging her just as possessively, no space between them, and he kissed her, their mouths melding, fulfilling the need to feel utterly deeply united, not wanting it to end.

This was it—she and Tommy—and surely nothing could ever part them now. The frustrations of the past...what did any of them matter? This was a new beginning—a beautiful, mutually felt beginning—that would cast its power over everything else.

Passion eased into a lovely sense of peace. Yet once their breathing became less laboured, and their hearts stopped racing, some cooler sanity trickled through the beautiful buzz of basking in their togetherness, bringing with it the realisation of where they were and where they should be…in attendance at the marquee until Miranda and Nathan took their leave.

"We can't just stay here, Tommy," Sam whispered.

"Mmmh…I'm willing to move…" He trailed his lips over hers "…as long as you promise…" soft, butterfly kisses "…this will be continued…when our duty's done."

"I promise," she answered on a rush of pure happiness.

He hitched himself up on his elbows and his eyes were deep, dark whirlpools of feeling, sucking away any doubts she might have about where they were going from here. "Having you means more to me than anyone's wedding. Tell me you believe that."

She wound her arms around his neck and smiled her implicit faith in the desire they shared. "I'm not about to let you go, Tommy. It feels as though I've been waiting all my life to have you."

He grinned. "You can say that again. For me."

Somehow that claim and the flashing dazzle of his smile came too quickly, too easily, niggling at her sense of rightness. "What about…" She instantly bit her lip, stopping the criticism and pushing it into the past where it belonged.

"The other women I've wasted my time with?" he picked up, his mouth twisting into an ironic grimace. "Something was always missing. But not this time. Not with you, Samantha. You're the woman with everything. Understand?" he softly appealed.

She wanted to accept it, had to, or what she'd just

felt with him would be diminished and *it had been perfect*. "Yes," she breathed on a contented sigh.

He nodded. "So keep this memory of us shining brighter than anything else until we're free to make it all we want. Okay?"

"Okay."

He pressed a feather-light finger to her lips, as though sealing her promise. "Then I guess we'd better get dressed and show our faces again."

Faces! She jack-knifed up, clapping her hands to her cheeks in dismay as Tommy rolled off the bed. "What will I do? I must have ruined all the make-up. And my hair!"

Having landed on his feet, Tommy turned and hauled her up to stand in his embrace, his grin a mile wide and his eyes sparkling warm approval. "Your hair is glorious just as it is. All tousled and sexy. And you don't need make-up. A bit of lipstick will make you respectable enough for the rest of the party."

"Are you sure it'll be all right?"

He laughed. "If you mean…will people take one look at us and know we've been making love…so what? I'm in the mood to trumpet it to the whole world."

Making love… Such wonderful, warming words! She thought fleetingly of Janice Findlay's remark about "feeling horny." Making love was something very different, and suddenly, like Tommy, she didn't care if the whole world knew. Though they didn't have to be told.

"Don't you dare brag, Tommy King!" she cautioned.

His eyebrows rose. "Are you asking me to hide what I feel for you?"

She flushed all over with pleasure. "No. I just meant…"

"What's private to us is private to us," he interpreted, touching his finger to her nose with tender indulgence. "Don't worry, Samantha. I'm not a crass playboy who parades his prowess with women. And what I have with you, my darling, belongs to me. No one else."

Sam sighed contentedly. His darling. She knew they should be getting dressed, getting back to the marquee, but when he kissed her, she just wanted to kiss him back, revelling in belonging to him like this, feeling securely wrapped in his warm strength, their naked bodies rubbing together, nothing coming between them.

It was Tommy who stopped it, growing aroused again and warning her, "If you don't want to be back on that bed…"

"We'd best get into our clothes," she finished with reluctant resignation.

"And tempt me not," he added wickedly.

She laughed and broke away, delighted she *could* tempt him. Her whole body tingled with the pleasure of his lustful watching as she busied herself, trying to look like a bridesmaid again. It felt very intimate, dressing themselves in full view of each other. Like a husband and wife, she thought, though they were only lovers, as yet.

Fortunately the beautician had left her an array of cosmetics so she could do a fair job of repairing her make-up. The only option with her hair was to brush it out, but since Tommy stood behind her, avidly running his fingers through the riot of curls, she didn't mind at all how it looked. He loved her hair, loved *her*... So what did anything else matter?

They left the house, hand in hand, and the night sky was full of brilliant stars. Sam had never felt so happy in her life. It was as though this night was made especially for her and Tommy, and even the sky was twinkling in celebration of their coming together.

As they strolled down the lawn, rollicking music was pumping out of the marquee, the guests were clearly getting boisterous, and Sam decided she and Tommy wouldn't have been missed at all. "What time is it?" she asked, realising the party mood had definitely elevated since they'd been gone.

He checked his watch. "Half an hour to go before Miranda and Nathan take their leave." He grinned at her. "We'll make the last show, no problem."

The reception was due to end at 1:00 a.m. Tomorrow morning there would be a big buffet breakfast, after which Miranda and Nathan would fly off to their honeymoon and the guests would make their way home.

Tommy squeezed her hand. "I want you to stay on here with me tomorrow. Will you?" His dark eyes simmered with promises yet to be spoken.

"Yes," she answered simply, discarding her earlier decision to fly home with her family.

They smiled at each other, their new understanding putting a golden glow around her heart.

"Well, well, look who's here, Greggie! Your little sister with her hair all tumbled, and Tommy the tom-cat wearing a satisfied smile," came the slurred and sexily suggestive voice of Janice Findlay.

It jerked Sam's gaze towards the clump of trees some ten metres from the marquee. From amongst the shadows Tommy's ex-lover lurched from a clinch with Greg, her black dress sagging over one shoulder, baring even more of her cleavage.

"Oh! Hi, Sam!" Greg acknowledged sheepishly, catching Janice around the waist to support her against him.

Tommy exhaled between his teeth but held his tongue, choosing to avoid any altercation. He quickened his pace, pulling Sam with him, intent on not getting involved with the necking couple. Sam dragged her feet, disturbed by her brother's attachment to Tommy's ex-lover.

"Go and get us a bottle of champagne, Greggie, darling," Janice urged. "Let's have our little orgy in style."

She patted his face indulgently, making Sam cringe inwardly, then gave him a shove towards the entrance to the marquee.

"Orgy and bubbly," he said, beaming at Sam and Tommy as he rambled off to do Janice's bidding.

"He's drunk," Sam whispered in some concern.

"So's she," Tommy muttered back.

"Should we do something?"

"Like what? They're both over the age of consent."

"Not so hot to trot now, Tommy?" Janice jeered, staggering towards them.

"She'll fall," Sam worried, stopping their progress towards the marquee.

"Got her, didn't you?" Janice went on. "Get 'em all. Snap o' your fingers. Fall like ninepins for a guy like you."

Tommy heaved an exasperated sigh. "Why don't you take better care of yourself, Janice?"

She laughed derisively. "You don't care. Left me knocked up and don't give a damn! Won't even give me time of day."

Shock punched into Sam's heart, smashing the golden glow to smithereens.

"I beg your pardon," Tommy bit out tersely.

"Preggers. Bun in the oven," Janice elaborated, jabbing an accusing finger at him. "Your little bastard, Tommy King."

Was it true? Sam darted a pleading glance at Tommy, willing it to be a spiteful lie.

"Oh, no it's not!" came his swift and vehement denial. "Don't think you can tie that on me, Janice, because I won't wear it. I took better care of you than you did yourself."

"Slipped up then, didn't you?"

"Not a chance."

Janice turned her drunken venom on Sam. "See what a sleaze he is? Bet he's got little bastards he won't own up to all around the Outback. Probably planted one in you tonight."

"That's enough!" The words cracked from Tommy like a bullwhip.

Janice rocked back and forward on her feet, her eyes rolling out of any steady focus.

Sam stood chilled to the bone, not knowing what to believe and too frightened to think about what any of this meant.

"I'd advise you to think very soberly about being sued for slander if you repeat what you've just said to anyone else," Tommy threatened, his voice as hard and cold as steel.

Janice's eyes narrowed on him. "I'm gonna slap a paternity suit on you."

"If you expect to gain anything from this, you're badly mistaken. What you need is some help before you make everything worse for yourself."

"If you're telling me to get an abortion…"

"I'm telling you you need counselling to get your life straightened out. You're off your head with alcohol half the time and don't know what you're doing."

"Do so!" Her chin went up and her face took on a smug look of animal cunning. "You got *her*." She sneered at Sam. "I got her brother. And maybe I'll load him with your child. How do you like them apples?"

"You reveal yourself for what you are, Janice," Tommy answered with biting distaste. "Nothing but a lying bitch!"

It turned her ugly. "Well, you didn't mind lying with me, lover. And Greg Connelly's lining up for it." She sliced a look of contempt at Sam. "Neither of them are any better than me, so take that on board, little sister.''

''Got the bubbly!'' Greg called triumphantly, drawing their attention. He was waving the bottle over his head as he ambled towards them. ''Glasses, too,'' he added, holding them up like trophies.

''What a good boy you are!'' Janice drooled sickeningly. Then tossing a venomous, ''Stuff, you two!'' at Tommy and Sam, she swayed her way over to Greg, threw her arms around his waist and fondled him back to the cover of the trees, giggling and teasing in a pointed demonstration of how on top of the game she was.

''I'm Greg's big sister, not his little one,'' Sam corrected anxiously. ''I should stop this before he gets into trouble.''

''Leave them be! He won't thank you for it,'' Tommy answered tersely.

''But...''

''He's a man.'' Angry eyes shot daggers into hers. ''Haven't you learnt anything?''

It took Sam's breath away. However faulty her judgment about men might have been in the past, was this fair comment when her brother was being manipulated into a possible scandal? A very female rage started burning, Janice's snide words beating through her brain—*neither of them are any better than me.*

It was Tommy who had started this, blithely falling into an ill-judged affair with Janice Findlay, seeking satisfaction without caring about consequences. Her eyes blazed back into his as her own fierce resentments erupted.

"Am I supposed to respect a man who blinds himself to what he's taking on for the sake of a bit of easy sex?"

His face stiffened. "You respect his right to make his own choices."

"So how do you like your choice now, Tommy? What if Janice is pregnant to you?"

"She's not."

"How can you be sure?"

"You heard her!" he flung back impatiently. "This is nothing but a malicious tit for tat because I chose to be with you rather than pick up with her again."

Could the whole nasty encounter be dismissed so easily?

Tommy dropped her hand and grabbed her upper arms. Sam thought he was going to shake her, but his fingers merely pressed urgently into her soft flesh. "Are you going to let her win?" he demanded. "Can't you see it's what she wants...to spoil what there is between us?"

Sam sucked in a deep breath. Doubts were swirling through her mind. A new beginning, a new beginning, she recited frantically, trying to hold on to what she had felt before Janice had injected her poison. Tommy was hers now. A dream come true. But was it ever possible to be free of past actions? They had such long tentacles, and the longest one of all would be a child Tommy had fathered with another woman.

Anguished by the possibility, she asked again, "How can you be sure she's not pregnant to you?"

He huffed his vexation with the question. "It's been over three months since I was last with her. Why wait until today to deliver the news?"

Sam frowned. The timing did seem wrong.

"Janice was peeved by my earlier brush-off and determined to do maximum damage to us," Tommy argued, anger still pumping from him. "It's as simple as that, Samantha."

Was it?

"If she's in an alcoholic fog half the time, maybe she didn't realise her condition until very recently," Sam reasoned. "She could have thought today might be a good day to approach you on it."

"My brother's wedding day?" Tommy reminded her, his voice laced with acid scepticism.

"She might have wanted to test how approachable you were," Sam argued, thinking it couldn't be an easy thing to tell a man who'd dumped you he was the father of an unplanned child.

And Tommy had cut Janice dead.

Wouldn't that give rise to vengeful impulses?

"You're worrying over nothing," he insisted dismissively. "Apart from the time factor, I always used protection with Janice. With every woman I've ever been with, in fact."

Not with me! The memory sliced straight through his argument with devastating force. He hadn't used protection with her. Hadn't thought of it. Neither of them had.

"There's absolutely no chance she's pregnant to me. I swear it, Samantha."

But how could she believe him? Might there not have been a time with Janice when he hadn't stopped to think? When he, too, was the worse for drink after a party?

"Now put it out of your mind," he commanded. "It's not worth another thought, I promise you." He released her arms and drew her into a hug at his side, walking her forward towards the entrance to the marquee. "Time we made our appearance and checked in with Nathan and Miranda," he said with determined authority.

That, at least, was true.

Sam let herself be carried along with him but it felt as though the stars had winked out and a dark cloud had settled over their future together.

Tommy hadn't used protection tonight.

Was that a first with him...because he was with her? Because it was different from his usual playboy affairs? Because she was the one woman he really wanted to spend his life with?

Sam wanted to believe it.

She wanted to believe Janice was lying.

But what if she wasn't?

CHAPTER ELEVEN

SHE WASN'T convinced.

Tommy knew it and cursed himself for being all kinds of a fool. He could feel fine little tremors running through Samantha's body and her submission to his lead, to the closeness he pressed on her with his hug, had nothing to do with wanting to be with him, more the aftermath of shock.

Janice's malevolent spite had broken the intimate understanding between them.

No, damn it! *He* had. For having the monumental stupidity to get involved with Janice Findlay in the first place. And not being kinder to her today. The urge to protect and pursue what was developing between him and Samantha had overriden a more tactful rejection, but he sure as hell was reaping the consequences now.

Then to have lashed back at Samantha about respecting a man's choice...utter madness! In the light of what had happened tonight—how he felt with her—*he* couldn't respect any of his previous choices, so why should she? Especially his affair with Janice.

Though she wasn't—couldn't be—pregnant to him. He didn't have to give that a second thought. But how was he going to get the doubt out of Samantha's head?

The truth was he'd been a blind idiot all these

years, fooling around with women who didn't hold
a candle to Samantha Connelly, and those ghosts
were swirling with a vengeance right now. Why
should she take his word that he'd always been responsible about contraception? She was probably remembering he hadn't used anything with her tonight.
The moment had been too big to think of precau-
tions. Did she understand how much it meant? That
it was driven by needs that went beyond the merely
physical?

How could he prove it when she'd just been
slapped in the face by his undeniable sexual intimacy
with Janice Findlay? And he'd topped that by more
or less approving Greg's pursuit of it, too. And why?
Because he'd wanted Janice out of *his* hair, wanted
to get Samantha away from her. No noble ideals
about the right to choose in that decision!

He stopped, riven by guilt. They'd reached the entrance to the marquee and the party beckoned, but he
had to show Samantha he did have some decency.
"You go on inside," he said. "I'll find Greg and
have a word with him. Sort things out."

Slowly, she turned her gaze up to his, her beautiful
blue eyes clouded with painful confusion. "You
said…"

"I was wrong. If Janice is making Greg a scape-
goat for my sins, he ought to know about it."

"He probably won't thank you," she acknowledged with a wobbly grimace.

"Better an informed choice than an uninformed
one," he conceded dryly. He reached up and stroked
her cheek in tender reassurance. "I'm sorry for let-

ting my anger at Janice's accusation spill over onto you. It is a lie, Samantha, so please...don't let it come between us.''

Relief...hope...uncertainty....

''Save the last dance for me,'' he said with persuasive force, willing her to have more trust and confidence in him by the time he returned to her side.

Sam didn't move forward as Tommy left her. She felt incapable of making any decision about what she should do. At least the worry about her brother was eased and she was grateful for that.

She stared blankly at the party scene in front of her, too churned up inside to feel drawn to it. Her mind kept jagging over what had just transpired. People did do and say mean things out of spite and frustration, she reflected, especially when pride was wounded and envy was eating away at one's heart. She was guilty of it herself with Tommy. Maybe Janice did just want to do damage and it was wrong to let her win.

Her head was beginning to ache and the noise level around her didn't help. The drummer of the band was giving a virtuoso performance. It felt as though he was beating her brain...boom, crash, rat-a-tat-tat! She wished he'd stop.

''Sam?'' A hand on her arm...Elizabeth...concern in her eyes. ''Are you all right?''

She managed a wan smile. ''Bad headache.''

''Ah...were the pins in your hair too tight?''

Sam gratefully seized on the excuse. ''I guess I

wasn't used to them. I took them out. I hope Miranda won't mind."

Elizabeth nodded to the dance floor, dryly commenting, "I doubt Miranda is seeing anything but Nathan right now. They'll be making their departure soon."

"Yes, I knew I had to be here for that."

"If you feel really ill…"

"No. It's all right."

A searching look showed doubt but she didn't press the issue. "I thought I saw Tommy come in with you."

"Yes. There was a bit of trouble outside. He decided he'd better sort it out, but he'll be right back. In time for…"

"What trouble?"

"It's nothing really," Sam hastily assured her. "I was worried about Greg. He's…well…under the weather…and Tommy's gone to help him. A man-to-man talk. That's all."

"Ah!"

Elizabeth's satisfied nod was sweet relief to Sam. She quickly changed the subject. "We met Christabel Valdez earlier. Jared seems to be very struck on her."

The all too shrewd gaze travelled back to the dance floor, targeting the son who worked with her and the woman who was keeping her distance from him even as they danced. Jared's face was lit with warm pleasure in his partner. Christabel's expressed a lively interest. Whether the interest was polite or deeply personal was impossible to tell.

"What do you think of her?"

The question surprised Sam. Elizabeth King was the kind of person who usually kept her own counsel, though she had spoken very personally to her earlier today. Flinching away from that memory and its on-the-mark advice, Sam concentrated hard on what was being asked, flattered that her opinion might be valued by Tommy's mother.

It was on the tip of her tongue to say Christabel was definitely not of Janice Findlay's ilk, but she bit back the too revealing remark. "I think she's a very together person inside. What she does is for herself. I liked her," she simply said.

"Yes. It's as though she's deliberately limited her needs," Elizabeth mused slowly.

Or perhaps Christabel's needs were simple. She seemed to have led a complicated life, moving from country to country, possibly shedding everything but the bare essentials to her along the way. That made sense to Sam. Although being alone, far from any family seemed a strange choice. On the other hand Christabel might be like Miranda, with no family at all.

"Do *you* like her?" It was the more important question, Sam thought, if Jared was seriously attracted to the beautiful Brazilian. He was very close to his mother, in every sense, and would surely want her approval of his choice of partner.

"There's nothing not to like. Which makes me wonder why she works so hard at it." The cryptic remark was followed by a dismissive shrug. "It's up to Jared to work it out. If he wants to enough."

Respect for choices, Sam thought. Had Elizabeth drummed that into her sons? It was a fair philosophy to live by, as long as people were prepared to accept and shoulder the consequences of those choices, because there was no escape from them. There was no clean slate.

"Christabel has a child."

The quiet statement of fact hit a mountain of raw places in Sam. A child that was not Jared's, Elizabeth meant. And what might *she* be faced with—a child of Tommy's that was not hers!

She closed her eyes, unbearably pained by the thought. How could he walk away from that? A child...a little boy...or girl...carrying his genes. It would never feel right...never!

Please, God, don't let it be true, she prayed fervently.

"Is the headache worse?"

Elizabeth's anxious question jolted her eyes open again. "No," she denied before realising she would have to explain. "Just thinking," she added, her mind working feverishly to get back on track with Elizabeth's. "It must be hard being a single mother."

"Yes. Though it didn't start that way." She looked back at the dance floor, watching the woman they were discussing. "Christabel was married. She's a widow."

Widowed...maybe she was still grieving for her first love, which could explain the distance she now kept with men. Even attractive men. Christabel could be a one-man woman, like herself with Tommy—always an empty place that no one else could fill.

Poor Jared, if that was the case. He could be travelling a path to nowhere.

"Is Christabel's child a boy or a girl?" she asked, wondering how Jared was handling that situation—a child by another man. At least, the biological father was no longer physically there. Janice would be.

"A little girl." Another flat statement of fact, no expression in her voice—judgment reserved.

The child would never be a blood granddaughter to Elizabeth, Sam thought. Whereas if Janice had Tommy's child, it would be a King, and never would Elizabeth turn her back on any grandchild of Lachlan's. It would always have a place in the family. And rightly so. The next generation...

Oh, it was wrong, wrong, wrong. A child should be born of a love like Miranda's and Nathan's. Whatever Tommy had felt with Janice was gone. Yet such unplanned births did happen, and it was impossible to ignore a child's needs, if one had any conscience at all.

"Does Christabel's daughter get on with Jared?" Sam asked, not really imagining otherwise. Maybe that was one need to be filled and Jared had a naturally kind nature.

"I don't know." There was an odd distance in Elizabeth's voice. "I haven't even seen the child. Christabel keeps her personal life very private."

She's worried, Sam thought. Worried about where this might lead for Jared. And I'm worried about whether I can share Tommy's future. He cares about me, she fiercely assured herself. He cared enough to look after Greg for me. Or did he go to have a more private word with Janice, out of my hearing?

The music stopped but no one left the dance floor. The couples just chatted together, waiting for the next number to begin. "This will be the last dance," Elizabeth murmured. "I hope Tommy won't be long." She swung her gaze back to Sam, sharply inquiring. "Was it bad trouble?"

"Still here, waiting for me!" Tommy's voice seemed to explode into the highly sensitive moment, sweeping away the question just as he swept Sam away from his mother, his highly charged energy an electrifying force that nothing was going to stop. "Last dance, Mum," he tossed back at her, and as though the band heard him and took their cue from him, they started up a slow jazz waltz.

The moment they stepped on the dance floor, Tommy wrapped Sam in his arms, pressing her so close the burning heat and steel muscle of his body was stamped on hers, like a brand of ownership he was determined on maintaining, no matter what. And the painful muddle in Sam's mind melted into a pool of wanting that went so deep, her arms simply wound themselves around his neck and locked him to her. This dance was hers, she thought fiercely. Whatever came afterwards, this last dance with Tommy was *hers*.

He didn't speak. She didn't, either. Their bodies did all the talking, clinging to the sense of togetherness, silently recalling and revelling in the intimate knowledge they'd given each other, their legs interweaving with a sexual awareness that was intensely erotic. The need—the desire—to be with him again—always be with him—was overwhelming.

Her fingers stroked the back of his neck, compelled to touch. The skin was damp there. So were his curls. Had he been running to get back to her, sweating on it? She could feel his heart thumping against his chest, his cheek rubbing against her hair, yearning emanating from every part of him, yearning for her. She was sure of it.

As she snuggled her head closer to his, she caught sight of Elizabeth watching them, smiling at them, happy satisfaction written all over her face. It was as though she was beaming at them... This is right...how it should be with these two. And Sam thought of how Elizabeth had spoken to her about Christabel, like a mother to a daughter, sharing a confidence about family matters... Tommy's mother trusting her and the long link of knowledge and understanding they shared.

The realisation crept up on her...Elizabeth *wanted* the link. That's why she had spoken so bluntly before the wedding, wanting both she and Tommy to leap over the barriers they had set between themselves. Had she sensed all along they had always really wanted each other?

Both of them such fools, if what Tommy had insisted was true—that she was the one special woman for him. And it had felt true. Still felt true, now she was in his arms again. So it had to work out right, didn't it? Somehow.

Sam shut down her mind and gave herself up to the pleasure of feeling...being with Tommy...the deliciously sensual harmony of their bodies moving in unison...music driving their feet, the rhythm of it pulsing through them...and this man she loved holding her as though he wasn't whole without her, his breath in her hair.

She wanted the dance to go on and on forever, feeding the dream she had fostered all these years...a partnership welded by love, unbreakable. The music stopped, but Tommy didn't let her go. She didn't move from him, either. They remained locked together, uncaring what anyone else thought.

"Ladies and gentlemen...that was the last dance," the master of ceremonies declared. "If you'll now form a circle to wish the bride and groom farewell..."

Tommy's chest rose and fell on a long sigh. "Ready to join the hordes?"

"I guess so," she murmured, reluctant to face reality again.

It was Elizabeth's voice that forced them into action. "Sam, here's your bouquet."

Bridesmaid! *Her* duty to look after the bouquets. Sam jerked out of Tommy's embrace. Elizabeth was smiling at them, holding both her bouquet and Miranda's. "Sorry. Forgot what I should be doing," Sam rushed out as she accepted hers.

"I'll give this to Miranda," Elizabeth said indulgently, her dark eyes sparkling pleasure in Sam's forgetfulness. "You and Tommy join up with Jared near the exit. It will get the guests moving."

Tommy retained an arm around her waist as they stepped off the dance floor. Sam quickly scanned the crowd, wondering if Greg and Janice had returned to the marquee, inwardly agitated at the thought that one or other of them might cause an unpleasant scene during the leave-taking. She couldn't see either of them.

"They're not here," Tommy murmured, attuned to her concern.

She darted an anxious glance at him. "You spoke to Greg?"

He shook his head. "I couldn't find them. I went back to where we last saw them, looked around, called out. They must have slipped away somewhere else, or didn't want to be found."

In a way it was a relief. Greg's pride would have been hurt. Angry and drunk, he might have thrown a punch at Tommy. Besides, she didn't want to think about Janice and what might have been said. Easier to postpone that issue right now.

"I just hope they don't blunder back inside before Nathan and Miranda leave," she muttered.

"I doubt they'll return at all," came the dry retort.

He was probably right, given their intention of indulging themselves in a private orgy. Though it did leave things unresolved. On the other hand, how could the pregnancy question *be* resolved unless Janice had medical proof with her, and if she'd had that, she would undoubtedly have waved it under Tommy's nose.

A lie.

A spoiling lie.

Sam didn't want what she now had with Tommy spoiled. Not tonight. Not any night. Besides, it wouldn't be morally wrong to...to go back to bed with him. It wasn't as though Tommy was married to Janice or even attached to her.

Except...would she feel really good about it, with the phantom of Janice's pregnancy hovering in her mind?

Sam silently wrestled with this dilemma as the leave-taking ceremony proceeded, Nathan and Miranda circling around everyone, kissing, hugging, shaking hands. There was much merriment over comments and advice tossed at them and she smiled and laughed with everyone else, doing her best to keep up a happy, well-wishing facade.

Since the family were gathered at the exit, with Sam next to Tommy, they were the last on the farewell circuit. Nathan gave her a big-brotherly hug and whispered, "You've got Tommy lassoed. Hold him down, Sam."

She blushed as he grinned knowingly at her before passing on to his brother. She didn't hear what he said to Tommy because Miranda was kissing her cheek and murmuring, "Thanks for being my friend, Sam. And good luck with Tommy. Hang in there."

Slightly dazed by their personal comments, Sam watched them complete the full round with Elizabeth. The band struck up a jazzy rendition of "Here they go, here they go, here they go..." and the guests sang and applauded loudly as the bride and groom slipped out into the night...their wedding night.

People milled around in the marquee, continuing conversations, finishing drinks, collecting belongings. The exodus towards arranged accommodations didn't start until well after Nathan and Miranda would have reached the homestead. Sam and Tommy were continually caught up with various groups of guests who wanted to express their pleasure in the events of the day.

Sam smiled and chatted and agreed with everyone, conscious that Tommy was at his charming best in his responses. He gave no sign of being at all perturbed by the nasty contretemps with Janice. It seemed, as far as he was concerned, that page had been turned and the book was closed on it.

Hold him down...hang in there... The advice kept echoing through her mind, pushing back the doubts and fears that had so tormented her. She had the man she loved at her side. It would be terribly self-defeating to indicate in any way that she didn't trust his word. It *had* been different with her tonight with so much feeling running between them. That was why he hadn't thought to use protection.

"Samantha..." It was her mother, glancing around the marquee worriedly as she asked, "...have you seen Greg anywhere?"

"He left earlier," Tommy answered smoothly.

Her mother frowned. "He should have stayed to farewell Nathan and Miranda."

"Tommy!" The loud hail distracted them.

"Here!" Tommy called, holding up a signalling arm as he turned to see who wanted him.

Jim Hoskins, the head park ranger from The Bungle Bungles, signalled back, then shoved his way through the guests who'd gathered close to the marquee exit, his haste transmitting a sense of urgency that spelled trouble. An instant tension held them still and silent for the few moments it took for him to reach them.

"An accident," he stated quickly. "Jeep hit a tree next to the road to the resort. Doc Hawkins is there. He and his wife were in my vehicle. Sent me back for you. Says they'll have to be flown to hospital."

"How many hurt?" Tommy rapped out.

"Two. Both unconscious. Doc suspects internal injuries and it must have happened some time ago. We didn't hear the crash. We just came upon them."

"Who is it? Who's hurt?" Sam asked, knowing a lack of identification would spread anxious alarm through all the guests.

Jim had been concentrating on Tommy, but now he looked at her, his eyes pained. "It's your brother, Sam. It's Greg. And Janice Findlay."

CHAPTER TWELVE

Shock gripped Sam's heart. She instantly fought it away. There was no time for shock, no time for anything but doing what had to be done. There was no ambulance service to call out here in the Kimberly cattle country. Whatever action was needed had to be organised here and now.

"Mum..." She addressed her sharply, jolting her out of shock. It was her firstborn son—Sam's closest brother—but that couldn't be dwelled on. "Would you find Dad and Pete? Get them together and...Jim..." She swung back to him. "...did you drive your vehicle down to the marquee?"

He nodded.

"You'll take my family to the accident site, won't you?"

"Sure!"

"And the Findlays," Tommy instructed. "Ask my mother to break the news to them, Jim."

"Right!" he agreed.

Tommy looked at Sam, his dark eyes intensely focused. "We'll need two planes. Nathan's, where the seats can be removed for cargo. And a six-seater."

"Dad's. He parked it near the hangar. No problem. I'll go to the airstrip, get them ready."

"You'll fly?"

"It's night flying. There's no one better."

A flash of admiration. "No one. I'll collect the station foreman, organise a stretcher team and the table-top truck to transport them to the airstrip. We'll send men to take the seats out of Nathan's plane. I'll fly the injured in. You fly the families. Okay?"

"Okay."

He squeezed her arm and was gone, striding off to take charge of the most immediate transportation operation. Jim was already making a beeline for Elizabeth. Sam swung her gaze back to check on her mother. She hadn't moved.

"Mum, can you manage? Do you want me to get Dad?"

Her glazed eyes clicked into focus, anguish pouring from them. "I'll do it. It's just...Greg..."

Sam's heart contracted again. She shut off a threatening whirl of emotion. "I know. But he needs us, Mum," she said with urgent emphasis.

"Yes." Her mother visibly pulled herself together. "I'll see you at the plane, Samantha. Your father left the keys in it."

"He always does."

"Go and do what you have to."

She went, driving legs that felt like jelly into purposeful movement. Jared joined up with her as she left the marquee. "Tommy said to accompany you, lend whatever help you need," he said succinctly.

Help and authority, Sam realised. "We need to commandeer one of the catering vans. Save running up the hill to other transport."

One of the vans roared off as they raced around

to the side of the marquee. "Tommy on his way. You two think alike," Jared noted, just as a waiter met them with keys to the other van. "Thanks, mate. I'll drive, Sam."

She veered towards the passenger side. Jared was already gunning the engine as she jumped in and slammed the door. The airstrip was on the other side of the homestead, beyond the machinery sheds. Jared wasted no time in getting them there.

"I'll get Dad's plane and taxi it out to the runway," Sam instructed him. "If you'll supervise the seat removal in Nathan's…"

"Sure! Are you okay?"

"Yes," she answered with unflinching determination.

And so she was, while ever action was required— cool, calm, efficient and effective, making no mistakes. The injured couple were carefully loaded into Nathan's plane. Tommy and Doc Hawkins took off with them. The families boarded Robert Connelly's, and Sam took off with them.

There was nothing she could do about Marta Findlay's hysterical weeping and wailing over her daughter's possible injuries except block it out as best she could. She was grateful for her own family's silent forebearance and support during the flight. They understood this was a waiting time they all had to get through.

The Kununurra airport and hospital had been alerted to deal with the emergency situation. Ambulances and other vehicles were waiting. Radio contact was constant. The moment Tommy's plane cleared the lit runway, Sam landed hers. Even so, the ambulances were already gone and Doc Hawkins with them by the time her passengers had alighted. Tommy was waiting to direct them to their transport.

Sam's father gripped his arm. "How are they?"

"Alive," Tommy assured him.

Sam saw her mother sag with relief and didn't realise she was sagging herself. Tommy stepped past her parents and wrapped her in his arms. "It's okay. You did it," he murmured, stroking her back comfortingly, injecting his own powerhouse of energy into her fading strength.

He directed both families to a waiting minibus which would take them straight to the hospital, then led Sam to his own personal vehicle, parked behind the KingAir office that handled the charter services. Her legs had gone to jelly again and she was grateful for the arm hooked around her waist, holding her up, keeping her going. She felt terribly tired, all of a sudden.

Tommy opened the passenger door and lifted her onto the seat. He even did the safety belt up for her. Strange...all these years of being so fiercely independent. Now Tommy was taking care of her and she didn't mind a bit. No pride involved. It was easy to simply accept he meant her well, easy to let him be the strong one, no competition at all.

He stroked her cheek tenderly before closing the door, his dark eyes locking briefly with hers, transmitting caring concern. "You can rest, Samantha. It's all up to others now."

Yes, it was, she thought. Her part was over. Yet

as the steely control she had held on her mind slid away, the feelings she had been holding at bay crowded in. It was all very well to be satisfied she had carried off the positive action needed *after* the accident. What about *before*...when she had done nothing to stop what should have been stopped?

Where did responsibility begin and end? She was older than Greg. But how could she have known he'd be stupid enough to drive a jeep when he was rolling drunk? Or had it been Janice behind the wheel?

"Who was driving?" she asked as Tommy settled on the seat beside her.

He looked at her, a sad gravity on his face. "I'd say Janice," he answered quietly. "They were both thrown out of the jeep on impact, but Janice was on the driver's side."

She shook her head at the foolish recklessness induced by too much alcohol. And Greg was no better, going along with the ride, letting a woman who wasn't fit to drive take control of a vehicle, especially an open jeep that offered no protection. It was totally reprehensible. Utter madness. And for what? The promise of sex on tap for the rest of the night?

How highly did men rate sex, she thought bitterly. Risking life and limb for it seemed crazy to her, but at Greg's level of intoxication, maybe he had felt invincible...having what he wanted virtually held out to him on a plate. Had it been like that with Tommy...just going with the urge wherever it led, regardless of consequences?

She didn't realise her hands were tightly clenched in her lap until Tommy reached across and covered one warmly with his own. "Don't torment yourself with *if onlys*," he gently advised. "More than likely, speaking to them would have made no difference to the course they chose. And *they* chose it, Samantha."

"Don't ask me to respect that choice, Tommy," she flashed at him. "Drinking and driving..."

"Is stupid, yes. But neither of us was there to stop it."

"I should have spoken. Should have told Greg he was nothing but a mark to Janice."

"How do you know she wasn't just a mark to him, Samantha? A one-night stand he relished having."

The quiet but pointed argument churned up all her earlier bad feelings. "Was that what she was to you?"

He grimaced. "Is that relevant? Whatever my affair with Janice was based on...it's in the past."

"*She* brought it up tonight."

He stiffened. "You want to lay blame at my door? It's all my fault? Is that what you're thinking?"

"I don't know how well the shoe fits, Tommy. Only you know that," she retorted, too worked up to monitor what she said.

"I see." He removed his hand. The warmth died, replaced by chilling pride as he added, "You don't trust my word."

He didn't wait for a reply. Grim-faced, he turned away, switched on the ignition, revved the engine, and accelerated out of the parking lot.

Sam closed her eyes, savagely berating herself for doing precisely what she'd told herself not to do. There could be no happy future with Tommy if she didn't trust him. Why was she plunging down this destructive path? How stupid could she get? He'd answered all the stuff about Janice. Raking over it again only drove this horrible wedge between them and she didn't want it there. She wanted *him* and how he'd been towards her a few minutes ago...kind, caring, supportive.

The dark tension in the Range Rover as they drove to the hospital tore at her nerves. Guilt added its painful claws. She should be thinking of Greg, willing her brother to pull through, not fighting with Tommy over blame or anything else. Besides, it wasn't his fault. He hadn't drunk himself silly. He hadn't got behind the wheel of that jeep. He hadn't smashed it into a tree.

He had, in fact, gone to try to sort things out with Greg and Janice, and they might very well have deliberately ignored his calling out to them. She had absolutely no reason to cast Tommy as the prime mover of this wretched string of events. What went on inside other people's minds was driven by many things. And her mind, at the present moment, was a mess.

At this early hour of the morning, the parking lot at the hospital was sparsely occupied. Tommy drove straight to a bay near the emergency entrance. The minibus which had come in ahead of them was empty, both families already inside the building, waiting for news. Sam's heart clenched at the prospect of that wait. Tommy was right. There was nothing more they could do, but that knowledge didn't allay the fear of what might be happening.

The Range Rover came to a halt. As Tommy switched off the engine, a great welling of urgency turned Sam towards him. "I'm sorry." She reached out to touch him, to draw his attention to her. "It was wrong of me to...to..." She shook her head in anguish over her erratic emotions. "It's not your fault. I know it's not. I'm sorry I..."

"It's okay," he broke in gruffly. "I'm sorry, too. We've come through a lot in the past twelve hours...feels like a lifetime." His mouth curved into a wry smile. "Hard to balance a whole lifetime and get a perfect outcome when the factors are confused by other things."

She released a long, tautly held breath. "I want to trust you," she whispered, pleading his understanding.

He nodded. "Give it a chance, Samantha. Give *us* a chance."

"I want that, too. I've wanted it for so long, Tommy, it scares me. Like it can't really be true. Like something's going to smash it or take it away or make it wrong."

He undid his safety belt and leaned over, cupping her face, his eyes blazing with an intensity of feeling that demanded she focus on him...only him. "Nothing can make this feel anything but right," he murmured, and kissed her...kissed her with such passionate fervour, everything else was driven out of her mind.

She responded with a desperate hunger for the dream to come true...she and Tommy bonded together by love for the rest of their lives. The heat of desire swept away the cold reality of where they were, and why. This was a life-force that needed affirmation here and now, needed nurturing and growth. For a little while the dark clouds of the night were banished and only the two of them existed, pouring positive energy into each other.

"Hold on to the thought of us, Samantha," Tommy commanded huskily, his lips lifting away from hers. "I'm here for you. Understand? Whatever else happens this night, promise me..."

He stroked the tumbled curls away from her brow. She opened her eyes, the banked passion in his voice alerting all her senses to the import of what he wanted of her. Their kiss had re-energised every nerve and flooded her with warmth and hope and faith in their feeling for each other.

"Promise me..." he repeated, his dark eyes glowing like fiery coals "...you won't *let* anything get in the way of sharing with me all we can share."

"My family might need me," she reminded him.

"Through this crisis, yes," he agreed. "And I'll support you all I can. I meant for you to keep believing there's more to what we started today, Samantha. Much more."

She sighed, her heart warmed by the reassurance that he really did see a very definite future in their relationship. "I'm here for you, Tommy," she blurted out. "I always have been."

And that was the honest truth.

He sighed, too. "That's good to hear." With a wry little smile, he asked, "Do you want to go in now?"

No, she didn't. She wanted to stay with him. But

she quelled the selfish need and answered, "They'll be expecting me."

He nodded, unfastened her seat belt, and swivelled to alight from his side of the Range Rover. Sam didn't wait for him to open her door. More conscious now that her parents would welcome the comfort of her presence, perhaps even anxious for her to join them, she swung herself out of the vehicle, closed the door and was relieved to find her legs performing as firmly as they should.

Hand in hand, she and Tommy walked into the hospital, the bouyant feeling of being harmoniously linked with him unshaken by the clinical surroundings and what had to be faced. They found her family and the Findlays in a facilities room where mobile patients could go and make a cup of tea or coffee. It contained a kitchenette, dining setting, a couple of sofas, a bookcase and a television set.

Pete and her parents were seated at the table, hunched over coffee mugs and a plate of untouched biscuits. Ron and Marta Findlay were huddled on one of the sofas, Marta's head resting limply on her husband's shoulder, both of them looking totally worn out. They were all still dressed in their wedding finery, an incongrous touch, given the grim situation.

"Heard any news?" her father asked Tommy.

"No."

"They took them for X-rays."

"We should know something soon then."

Sam sat next to her mother and Tommy moved on to speak to the Findlays. Pete got up to make both of them coffee, glad to have something to do. The waiting was oppressive. It made any attempt at conversation feel stilted, forced. Speculation was futile. Until they knew the extent of Greg's and Janice's injuries, no plans could be made. Everything hinged on hearing something definite.

Tommy mentioned that accommodation had been booked for both families at the Kununurra Lakeside Resort. This information evoked grateful murmurs. Rest would be needed, sooner or later, and returning to King's Eden was not an option tonight. Sheer fatigue was already casting its pall over the tension of waiting, eyes drooping, bodies slumping.

At last Doc Hawkins appeared, his entrance acting like an electric shock, jolting them into a hyper alertness. He was in his fifties, grey-haired, lean and rather sharp-featured, but he had kind eyes and a gentle manner that inspired confidence.

"They'll mend. Both of them," he announced, instantly relieving them of their worst fears.

The tense stillness was broken. Everyone stirred, stretching tired and aching muscles.

"So what are the problems?" Sam's father asked, rising to his feet, ready to meet them head-on.

"Well, no cranial fracture or spinal damage, but they are both badly concussed. That will need watching for a couple of days."

"Greg's left leg?"

"Broken in two places. He also has three cracked ribs. No serious internal injuries, but quite a lot of deep bruising. The scalp wound needed stitching. Other cuts and abrasions have been dressed. He'll be sore and sorry for himself for quite some time but the healing should not be complicated.''

''Thank God!'' Sam's mother whispered, her eyes welling with tears. ''Can we see him?''

''Shortly. Though don't expect to speak to him.''

''What about Janice?'' Ron Findlay demanded gruffly, also on his feet, wanting action.

Doc Hawkins turned to him with a sympathetic grimace. ''I'm sorry to say it will be a longer haul for your daughter. Apart from the superficial injuries, her right arm and hip are broken. There is some internal damage. Nothing life-threatening to her but...''

''But what?'' Marta demanded shrilly.

In a quiet, grave voice, Doc Hawkins delivered the bombshell that was to shatter the soothing effect of his previous words.

''There was nothing we could do to save it. The bleeding...'' He shook his head sadly, sighed and simply stated, ''She lost the baby.''

CHAPTER THIRTEEN

BABY!

For a moment, Tommy's mind went blank with disbelief. Shocked incredulity was swiftly followed by a violent inner surge of protest. It wasn't true. It couldn't be true. He pushed up from his chair at the table, needing to face Doc Hawkins, needing to refute what he'd claimed. His whole body was in revolt against the idea that Janice *had been pregnant*.

"What baby?" Marta Findlay cried in bewilderment.

It snapped his head towards her. Marta's face reflected his own mental turmoil as she struggled up from the sofa, pulling at her husband's arm in an agitated need for answers she could understand.

"Ron...Ron...do you know anything about this?"

"No, I don't." Having gathered his distressed wife into a comforting hug, he frowned at the doctor. "You say Janice was pregnant?"

"No doubt about it," came the firm reply.

Not to me, Tommy thought fiercely. He'd used protection. It had to be to someone else...someone careless, and probably as drunk as Janice, just as Greg had been tonight.

"She was about three months along," Doc Hawkins added.

Tommy felt as though someone had kicked him in

146

the stomach. *Three months!* Even as his mind fought
to deny it, the spectre of Janice carrying *his* child
clung, and the recollection of everything he'd said to
her today hit him like a series of sickening blows.
What if the protection he'd used had failed? Nothing
was a hundred percent certain.

"Three months," Ron Findlay repeated, strug-
gling to take in the fact that his daughter had not
confided in him or her mother.

"She should have told us," Marta wailed.

"I'm sorry it's come as a shock," Doc Hawkins
said sympathetically. "I didn't realise..." He sighed,
grimaced. "She probably wanted to work things out
with the father. Privately."

Why would Janice wait until today to tell him,
Tommy argued to himself, still pushing away the un-
acceptable. He *wasn't* the father. It felt totally wrong
to him. There had to be another answer. Yet...if he
was wrong...

"Three months..." Ron Findlay frowned over the
time span. His gaze suddenly lifted and targeted
Tommy. Without a doubt, Janice had not kept their
affair a secret. Awareness of the connection and cal-
culation on it were coming straight at him. "Do you
know anything about this, Tommy?"

His heart clenched. Impossible to deny knowledge.
And it would damn him...damn him in everyone's
eyes. Especially Samantha's. She'd heard it all from
Janice's own mouth and she would no longer believe
his defence, not in the face of this medical evidence.

He heard her chair scrape out from the table. He
swung to face her, desperate to stave off a rift be-

tween them. She stood up and there was a terrible dignity in her stiffened, upright stance. She looked straight at him and he knew she was in retreat from what they had shared tonight. Her blue eyes were glassy, projecting a flat challenge.

Tell them or I will.

To her it was a matter of integrity. No escape from it. No excuse for ducking what she would see as *his* responsibility. He had to bear the weight of Janice's accusation now, whether it was true or not. By cutting Janice off and branding her a liar, he was probably already an irredeemable skunk in Samantha's eyes.

He turned back to the Findlays, automatically squaring his shoulders, knowing he had to deal with the situation. "Janice told me earlier tonight that she was pregnant," he stated flatly. "Quite frankly, I didn't believe her. I thought she was playing games."

"Games!" Marta repeated shrilly, her eyes sweeping him with scathing contempt. "More likely it didn't suit you to believe her."

"When was this?" Ron demanded, his gaze flicking to Samantha, the inference clear that he'd observed how closely they'd stayed together throughout the wedding. "When precisely did Janice tell you?"

The timing damned him even further, inevitably linking him to what followed, Janice going off with Greg, the accident.

"Excuse me, please," Samantha broke in. "Doc, I think this is private business between Tommy and

Mr. and Mrs. Findlay. Could you take us to Greg
while they're sorting things out?''

''Yes. Yes, of course,'' he quickly acceded, waving the Connelly family forward.

Tommy watched her go. She skirted the other side
of the table to where he stood, clearly demonstrating
a disinclination to even pass by him. There was to
be no standing by her man from Samantha Connelly,
he thought with bitter pride, though to be scrupu-
lously fair, could he expect her to?

He would have stood by her.

Come hell or high water he would have stood by
her!

She followed her parents and brother out of the
room without so much as a backward glance at him,
leaving him to face the firing squad alone. Not worth
listening to. Not worth defending. Not a word or a
look from her to show he was still worth something
to her. Just walking out of his life as though he meant
absolutely nothing. Zero.

''I'll be straight back to take you to Janice,'' Doc
Hawkins assured them before bowing out and tact-
fully closing the door.

Tommy tightened his jaw as he turned back to the
Findlays. There was a lot he would take on the chin,
but he wasn't about to be heaped with more guilt
than was his due. Ron and Marta wanted truth from
him. They'd get it, along with a few truths about their
daughter.

Janice was not fighting for her life.

The baby....his mind sheered away from thinking

about that loss...what might have been. He didn't know—still didn't know—if it had been his child.

What he did know was he could lose more than a child tonight.

Sam didn't quite know how she made it out to the corridor. Her head was buzzing as though it had been invaded by a swarm of bees. She felt too sick to even try to drive them out. Sick and faint and stupid for believing Tommy. For wanting to believe him.

The Playboy King.

For all she knew he had fathered other children on women he'd been with, as Janice had snidely suggested. He might well have fathered one on her tonight. And that definitely gave the lie to his claim of always using protection. Would he deny their child, too, if she'd conceived? Would he treat her as he'd treated Janice when he fancied someone else?

Sam felt herself swaying and reached out to prop herself against the wall. Black dots were dancing before her eyes and her face felt clammy. Doc Hawkins had passed her, striding ahead to lead the way to wherever Greg was. If she just rested a few moments, she would be able to catch up.

"Sam!" Her father's voice, calling to her thickly.

Her vision was wavering but she saw them all stop and look back at her. "Coming," she forced out, and tried to wave them on.

It must have been a limp, inept gesture, because her father ignored it. He backtracked so fast, Sam suddenly found herself scooped off her feet and cradled against his big barrel chest, relieved of having to take any further action.

"Pete, you go with your mother and check on Greg." His voice rumbled over her. "I'll be taking Sam outside. My little girl needs a breath of fresh air."

His little girl... Tears welled into Sam's eyes. The love in those words was her total undoing. She turned her face into her father's strong shoulder and wept for the loss of her dream. Impossible to have faith in Tommy's word anymore. He just said and did whatever would get him what he wanted.

Overwhelmed by her inner misery, Sam wasn't aware of how her father got her outside or even where they were...only that he sat down and held her on his lap, patting her back as he had whenever she'd been hurt in the long-ago days of her childhood.

"Sorry, love," he murmured, resting his cheek against her hair. "Had my mind on Greg. Wasn't seeing that you got hardest hit back there. Greg's going to be all right. But you..." His big chest rose and fell in a heavy sigh. "Tommy was always the one, wasn't he?"

"Yes," she choked out, snuffling into the comforting curve of his neck and shoulder, mindlessly wanting to be a little girl again, secure in a love that was always there for her. Her father had never let her down. Never.

"Looked like you finally had him roped tonight. Your mother and I were happy for you. I guess this business with Janice...well, it's upsetting. Wouldn't be the first time a couple made a mistake, though. Maybe…''

He was trying to make it better for her and Sam couldn't bear it. "No, Dad," she sobbed. "I was there when she told him she was pregnant and he was the father. He…he called her a liar. And I…I let myself believe him. I wanted to believe him.''

She burst into fresh tears, the anguish of her earlier uncertainties coming back in full force. Worse, because now she could feel it from Janice's side, the hell of being pregnant to a man who didn't want her anymore, who refused to even admit he could be the father…the wretched desolation of being faced with such an ungiving and unsympathetic attitude.

"There…there…'' her father soothed. "No doubt about her having been pregnant, but Tommy might not be the father, you know. Bit of a party girl it seemed to me…the way she was carrying on with Greg.''

"Oh, Dad!'' She shuddered as the fateful chain of cause and effect marched through her mind. "Tommy was so cold and cutting when she'd tried to talk to him earlier. I think Greg was…was a pride thing to Janice…hitting back at Tommy. And me, too, for taking his attention away from her.''

"Mmmh…hardly admirable behaviour. Maybe Tommy had cause to cut her dead if she'd played up like that with other men before. When he was going out with her. You shouldn't be too quick to judge him, Sam.''

She rolled her head in a painful negative. "I

can't...I can't excuse him anymore, Dad. There were...other things."

"Uh-huh. Want to tell me about them? Get them off your chest?"

"Won't help."

"Then just give it a rest. It's been a long day. A very long day. Too much to deal with in one go. Though let me say, I'm very proud of you...the way you held up and saw everything through. Very proud. Couldn't have asked more of anyone."

He kissed her forehead and ruffled her hair. "You're made of the right stuff, Sam. Your mother carries on about female frippery falderals but that doesn't count for much in my book. No...doesn't amount to much at all. It's what's in the heart that counts. You've got a heart as big as the Outback. And if Tommy King didn't recognise that tonight..."

Her body instinctively scrunched up, warding off the onset of more misery.

"But we won't talk about him," her father soothed. "We'll talk about the good times...eh? Don't know if I've told you this, but from the day you were born, you've been a joy to me, Sam. The best daughter a man could have. Always eager to have a go at everything. A real little braveheart, right from the start..."

Tommy was churning with urgency. He had to rescue something from this disastrous night, if it was only a stay of judgment. He couldn't bear the thought of having completely lost Samantha's respect. It wasn't right. She had to understand this wasn't a black and white situation. Damn it! He did have integrity. Never in his life had he weaselled out of responsibility for anything he'd done.

It came as another severe jolt to his system when he found none of the Connellys with Greg in the recovery room. Where were they? How long had he been with the Findlays? Driven by the fear of not having the chance to clear anything with Samantha, he shot back to the corridor and headed for the exit to the car park. If she left here tonight, still thinking the worst of him...

No, his mind fiercely dictated.

She'd promised she'd always be here for him.

The ghosts couldn't win now.

He wouldn't let them.

The exit door halted his rush for a moment. Then he was past it, breaking into a run. He saw Robert Connelly stepping up into the minibus, movement inside it.

"Wait!"

The big man stopped, stepped back onto the ground, and turned to face him. Relieved at having at least delayed the family's departure, Tommy dropped his pace to a purposeful walk, his mind racing over what to say to Samantha. However, instead of waiting by the minibus, Robert Connelly came to meet him, intent on intercepting whatever message Tommy was bringing.

"It's all right," he hastily assured Greg's father. "I just want to speak to Samantha."

"It's not all right, Tommy," he bruskly retorted,

taking a blocking stance. "You leave her be for now."

The hard-spoken command pulled him up. The look on Robert Connelly's face brooked no opposition. Tommy instinctively gestured an appeal. "You don't understand..."

"Yes, I do. You want my daughter...you clean up your act."

It rocked him. He scooped in a quick breath, frantically searching for a line of argument. "I swear to you it's not how it looks," he declared vehemently.

"I hope for both your sake and Sam's, it isn't, Tommy," came the level reply. "Your father was my greatest friend, and I can't believe that the kind of person Lachlan was didn't rub off on you...his bone-deep decency, his sense of honour..."

"You can add absolutely fair justice to that," Tommy whipped back, fiercely resenting the impugning of his character.

"Yes." Robert Connelly agreed, ploughing on with pointed intent. "And fair justice seen to be done. That was Lachlan's law. Don't tell me you've forgotten it."

Seen to be done. Even as the words were spoken, they hit home. He'd failed that test in front of Samantha.

"Whatever the rights and wrongs of tonight..." her father went on, "...they're yours to deal with. Don't drag my little girl through a mess she had nothing to do with. You understand me?"

"Yes. But will Samantha give me the benefit of the doubt in the meantime?" he argued, desperate for some foothold on the future he could see slipping away from him.

"Maybe time will help put things in perspective. I'll be taking her home with me tomorrow and I'm asking you to sort yourself out before taking up with her again. My Sam isn't one for you to trifle with, Tommy. I'll be coming after you with a gun if you play her false. Understand me?"

"I was *not* trifling with her. Nor would I," Tommy shot back at him.

"Just making sure you know what you're walking into if you walk back into Sam's life." He nodded to mark the end of the conversation. "We'll be going now. I'm hoping you can sort things out as well as your father used to. Needs doing, Tommy."

Having delivered that last piece of inarguable advice, Robert Connelly returned to his family and took them away, seeking respite from the traumas that had been inflicted upon them.

Tommy watched the tail-lights of the minibus disappear into the darkness with a heavy sense of fateful resignation. No sense in chasing after it. Robert Connelly was right. One couldn't force a future. One had to build it, and a shaky foundation didn't build a strong future.

Lachlan's law...the irony was he had recently cited it himself when he'd helped Nathan sort out a nasty situation that was hurting Miranda. He hadn't really thought about his father for a long time, probably because it was Nathan following in his legendary footsteps.

Still, he was one of Lachlan King's sons, and

proud of it, proud to have the legacy of his father's blood in his veins. He might not be a cattleman but in his own way, he'd pioneered a new industry in the Outback and he had no doubt his father would have applauded both his drive and enterprise.

But his more personal affairs...would they have won Lachlan King's approval?

Tommy took a good, hard look at himself.

The Playboy King.

What had that title won him?

Nothing of any real value. Nothing that would stick by him. Nothing but grief for the woman he really wanted.

The more critical question was...what had it cost him...and could he recover the loss he'd brought upon himself tonight?

CHAPTER FOURTEEN

CHRISTMAS day....

Sam felt none of the excited anticipation that waking up to this day would have once brought. She had no urge to leap out of bed to see if the rest of the family were up yet, and no wish to stir them into activity if they weren't. Putting on a happy face took considerable effort and it was easier to delay having to do it.

She lay quietly in the old brass bed that had always been hers, her gaze idly roving over the mementos of her childhood and adolescence. All the things she'd kept remained precisely where she had placed them. In a way, coming back here was like stepping into a previous life, though she herself hadn't really changed.

On top of the chest of drawers sat the beautiful doll her mother had given her when she was four. She'd never played with it, hadn't seen what use it was. Its long auburn ringlets were still tied with green satin bows, and the matching green satin dress with its frills and coffee-lace trim was in the same pristine state as it had been when the doll was given, twenty-four Christmases ago.

Hanging on the wall facing her were the ribbons she'd won at rodeos, riding Lightning in the barrel races. He'd been a great horse, the fastest sprinter she'd ever had and so quick at turning around the barrels, it was magic the way he responded when they were competing to win. She'd wept buckets when he died from an infection the vet couldn't fix.

But life moved on. Tragedies slid into the past and other things became more important. On the dresser was a photograph of herself holding her pilot's license, one of the proudest moments of her life. Flying a plane was more exhilarating than riding a horse; taking to the air, owning the sky...like Tommy.

She sighed to ease the tension in her chest. How long had it been now...six, seven weeks? A bit over seven. The wedding had been on the sixth of November. Tommy had made no attempt at contact with her since then. Though she did know from her mother that he'd visited Janice in hospital several times, dropping in on Greg, as well.

It had actually been easier for her when her mother and brother were away, the reminders of that dreadful night at a distance. Her father let her be and Pete minded his own business. With Greg back home and having to nurse his leg, he was more or less underfoot and wanting company. Both he and her mother kept bringing up Tommy, and as much as she tried to block any conversation about him, they still dropped loaded little comments, referring to their *togetherness* at the wedding.

They also pointedly informed her that the Findlays had taken Janice home with them to Cairns, a long way from Kununurra, right across the country to the east coast. Away from Tommy was the apparent implication, not that it mattered. Tommy had made it all too brutally clear he didn't want Janice in his life, and it was that callous brutality that stuck in Sam's mind. Greg didn't seem perturbed by the loss, either. Which clearly demonstrated what casual sex was worth. Nothing that lasted beyond the moment. Unless it resulted in an unwanted pregnancy.

It didn't really help that the pregnancy was no more.

All it did was put an end to that chapter in Tommy's life. A convenient end, she thought bitterly, given his attitude towards it.

As for the rest of his life…the rest of hers…despite everything, the torment continued to linger. Had she done the right thing, walking away from that night and all it had entailed? In sheer self-survival mode, she'd wrapped herself in a mental and emotional fog, automatically taking over the running of the Connelly homestead while her mother stayed on in Kununurra to be by Greg. She'd filled the days with chores, keeping so busy she fell into bed at night, too exhausted to think.

She didn't want to think about Tommy now, either. After Christmas would be soon enough. In the new year. When she'd have to make decisions about continuing to work for him or…her mind shied away from *or*. Best to get moving—out of bed, into a shower, clothes on. She would wear a dress for Christmas. It would please her mother.

It should have been a happy Christmas day, Elizabeth King thought, but it wasn't…quite…despite

Miranda's and Nathan's announcement this morning that they were expecting a baby. It was wonderful news—Lachlan's first grandchild—and Tommy had carried on exuberantly about becoming an uncle. But she'd seen the shadow of pain on his face before he'd switched on the positive energy expected of him.

He was very good at putting on a show.

And he'd kept it up during their festive lunch, with Jared supporting him, their witty banter keeping laughter rolling around the table. Both brothers were genuinely happy for Nathan and Miranda. Elizabeth wished they could be happy for themselves, but knew they were not.

Jared had asked her if he could invite Christabel Valdez and her daughter to King's Eden for Christmas. She'd readily given her assent, hoping he had not sensed her own misgivings about the relationship he obviously wanted. In fact, it was a curious move from him. There had never been any embargo on inviting friends to the homestead for Christmas festivities. Had he been subtly probing her reaction to the idea of having Christabel in the family circle on an intimate level?

Difficult to know with Jared. He had his own quiet way of manoeuvring pieces into position—a formidable player in the business world, but he wasn't emotionally involved when it came to cutting deals. Unrequited passion could wear patience and control very thin.

She didn't know if he had actually invited Christabel. Perhaps he'd thought better of it, not ready to commit himself so far, or realising the invitation might be rejected. Putting himself in a losing situation was not Jared's way. Nevertheless, he had to be feeling disappointment that Christabel was not here.

As for Tommy, Elizabeth feared the fallout from the Janice Findlay affair cut too deeply for him and Sam to come together again. She'd flown to Kununurra herself the Monday after the wedding. Sam had already left for home with Robert, a move which had spoken volumes even before Elizabeth had managed a heart-to-heart talk with Tess Connelly.

Time, they had hopefully decided, would put things right eventually. But time could also feed the demon, pride, Elizabeth thought now. Both Tommy and Sam had let pride be a bristling sword between them before. If they saw the climax of that night as a betrayal of each other, would either of them be prepared to risk their hearts again?

If the ghosts stay away, Tommy had said when he'd danced with her at the wedding, and Janice had undoubtedly raised many ghosts. The pity of it was…truth and justice didn't repair the hurt done to the victims of a crime. Nothing could bring back what had been destroyed. Yet, was real love ever completely destroyed?

Aware that Tommy had fallen silent at the table, Elizabeth surreptitiously observed him watching Miranda and Nathan. Jared had prompted them into discussing what names they favoured for a son or daughter. Their faces glowed with love and the pleasurable anticipation of having a child to name.

Tommy's jaw suddenly tightened. He pushed back his chair and stood up. "One last Christmas toast," he said, claiming everyone's attention as he picked up his glass and held it high. "If this is a day of peace and good will, let it be. Let it be," he repeated fiercely, and drank without waiting for anyone else to echo it.

They all watched him, somewhat startled by his abrupt change of mood. He set his glass down, swept them with a look of reckless purpose and announced, "I beg to be excused. I need to be elsewhere. And who knows?" He tossed them a devil-may-care smile as he headed out of the dining room. "I may bring back the gift of a lifetime."

"Sounds like a plane coming in," Pete remarked, killing conversation as everyone paused to listen.

It *was* a plane coming in.

Sam's heart fluttered, a wild hope zinging through her as she instantly connected the sound to Tommy. Her mind was slow to override the reaction. Why would Tommy leave King's Eden to come here on Christmas day? It made no sense. There was nothing to get excited about. Most likely it was someone lost, someone in trouble, needing help.

"I'll go and see who it is," she said, pushing up from the table, needing the activity to settle her out-of-control nerves. The wall clock above her father's head showed twelve minutes to three…midafternoon. Tommy was undoubtedly still sitting with his family over their festive lunch, just as she was. Once she'd identified the pilot, she could bury Tommy in the dark recesses of her mind again and not let him out for the rest of the day.

"Might as well all go," her father said, dragging his chair back and patting his tummy. "Need some exercise after that huge meal."

"You pigged out on the pudding, Dad," Pete teased, getting up to satisfy his curiosity.

"Christmas comes but once a year," her father declared. "Got to make the most of it."

The others laughingly agreed, moving to follow Sam as she headed for the verandah overlooking the airstrip. A rise of inner tension prevented her from laughing. She couldn't even act casually over who might be landing at the Connelly homestead. The compulsion to know drove her feet faster.

The plane touched down on the rough dirt runway as she pushed open the screen door to the verandah. Sheer impetus carried her to the railing which she instinctively gripped—a steady, external support for the inner turmoil raised by the sight of the small aircraft skimming over the ground in front of her.

No mistaking the big *K* on its tail.

KingAir printed clearly underneath it.

Could it be a charter? Or was it Tommy himself? And what would she do if it was Tommy?

Her mind jagged between a helpless wanting and almost violent rejection. Her heart felt torn. Her stomach had lost any semblance of a comfort zone. And her family emerged onto the verandah, completely relaxed and ready to welcome a visitor, outback hospitality about to be extended to whomever it was.

"See any identification on the plane?" Pete asked eagerly, watching it being turned around at the end of the runway.

No point in prevaricating. Sam worked some moisture into her mouth which had gone as dry as the land before the Big Wet. *"KingAir,"* she answered, trying to keep her voice emotionless.

"Tommy," her father said in a tone of satisfaction.

Every nerve in Sam's body tensed. She never had asked what her father had said to Tommy just before they'd left the hospital in the minibus. She'd simply been grateful to be spared any further conflict with him that night.

"Why do you think so, Dad?" she blurted out.

The plane was taxiing back to park near the homestead. Still, there was no absolute certainty about the identity of the pilot at the controls.

"Oh, it just seems like a good day for him to pick."

Her head jerked around, her gaze slicing hard and fast to her father's. "A good day for what?"

He shrugged. "Peace and good will," came the bland answer.

"Tommy was great visiting me in hospital and bringing me stuff," Greg remarked happily. "Think I'll go and meet him."

He stepped off the verandah.

"No! Wait!" Both the protest and the command burst off Sam's tongue, causing her brother to pause and look quizzically at her.

"What for?" he asked when she didn't follow up with a reason.

Panic was causing a shortness of breath. She didn't know what to do, what to say. She wasn't *prepared* for this!

"I think Sam has private business with Tommy, Greg," her father explained. "Might be best if she met him first...settle things between them."

"Oh!" Enlightenment spread into an arch look as he stepped aside to give her the right of passage. "Your move, big sis."

Which meant she had to move. Gritting her teeth, Sam forced her legs into action. Her father was right. If it was Tommy in that plane, better she met him out there, beyond earshot of her family, though there was no way they weren't going to view what went on. She could feel their interest burning into her back as she left them behind.

The plane came to a halt. Its engines were switched off. *It may not be Tommy,* she kept telling herself, trudging determinedly forward, her shoulders automatically squared and her head defiantly high. The heat haze of midafternoon made everything shimmer. She wanted to shade her eyes with her hand but it seemed like a weak action so she refrained from doing it. A fierce sense of pride quelled the inner panic. If this *was* Tommy, he could do the speaking. Then she'd know what to say.

The cockpit door opened.

Tommy King stepped out onto Connelly land.

Something punched Sam's heart. Her feet stopped

dead. He had come. He'd left his family Christmas at King's Eden and flown here…to her.

He stood where he'd stepped down, staring at her. Since she'd stopped several metres from him and he wasn't coming any closer, she couldn't see what was in his eyes yet she felt the intensity of their focus on her, the impact of it spreading electric tingles, igniting nervous mayhem.

She stared back, wishing he didn't have the power to affect her so much. Did nothing change it? Would she always feel like this with Tommy, as though the very vitality of her existence depended on him? She could cope without him but…she didn't want to. She simply didn't want to. He made life bright, exciting, challenging…and dark, and miserable and conflict-ridden, she savagely reminded herself.

There he stood, his playboy handsome face framed by the riot of black curls that seemed to embody an untamed spirit, his tall athletic body radiating energy and a strong, virile maleness that was loaded with sex appeal. And she was vulnerable to it, every bit as much as any other woman who'd fallen for it, but physical magnetism wasn't going to win her to his side. Not today. Not ever.

She wanted more than that from Tommy. Much more. If he thought she was going to cross this space between them and fall at his feet, he could think again. If that was what he was waiting for, he could wait until doomsday. It wasn't enough that he'd come this far for her. Her pounding heart demanded that he show her how much she was worth to him. In every way.

*   *   *

Tommy stood there, feeling her pull on every part of him, and the wanting that had been so briefly satisfied the day of Nathan's wedding, became more acute than it had been that night. He needed this woman. She answered things in him that no other ever had. Or would, he thought with painful irony, aware of how nearly his past had come to wrecking any future with her. And might still, if her mind had become completely set against him.

Funny…he hadn't considered her beautiful…all those years when he'd told himself other women were much more attractive, better-looking, sexier, and of course, appreciated the man he was more than Sam Connelly did. But she *was* beautiful. More beautiful to his eyes than all the rest.

She shone. Her hair was a halo of glory in the afternoon sunshine. He loved the sky blue clarity of her eyes, and the freckles she hated were endearingly girlish, stirring some protective streak in him. There was more appeal in her face than any supposedly classical beauty could strike.

She was wearing a blue petticoat dress that fired his memory of the soft, supple femininity of her body and the fierce tensile strength in her arms and legs, winding around him, binding him to the mutual possession that had felt so right, so perfect. The desire to feel it again seized him, but he knew he had to control it. He hadn't come for the body of Samantha Connelly. He knew she wouldn't give it unless she could give her heart, as well. That was what had to be won…won and kept.

Her approach to the plane had buoyed his hope

she was ready to be receptive, might even welcome him. Her abrupt halt at the sight of him put paid to that idea. Her rigid stance encouraged nothing. Pride set in stone, he thought, and felt his own pride start to bristle.

If she couldn't believe in him now…

If she wouldn't trust him…

He'd come this far. The risk had to be taken. He scooped in a deep, calming breath and walked towards her, purpose steeled in every stride.

There was no meeting him halfway but at least she didn't turn her back on him. She stood her ground. Her hands clenched as he came closer. Her eyes flared a warning, her chin tilted aggressively, and he knew she'd fight him if he crossed whatever line she'd drawn in her mind.

He only had one weapon that could cut through that line. Talking wasn't going to do it and touching was clearly a transgression she wouldn't tolerate. He had to gamble everything on the one possibility that might restore her faith in his word.

It went against his grain, having to accept that *his* word wasn't enough. He hadn't lied to her, not once. Yet there was no denying that circumstances had let loose the ghosts they had almost dispersed that night. No doubt they had been preying on her mind ever since.

He stopped short of her, ensuring she didn't feel threatened. Without saying a word he withdrew the envelope from his pocket and held it out to her, keeping a respectful distance. Her fiercely held gaze wa-

vered and slowly dropped to the slightly crumpled
piece of stationery.

. ''What's this?'' she demanded hoarsely.

''Just do me the courtesy of taking it and reading
what's inside, Samantha. It's self-explanatory.''

She unclenched her right hand, lifted it and took
the envelope. The tightness in Tommy's chest did
not ease at this act of co-operation. It was up to her
now...whether they'd share a future or not. All he
could do was wait.

Was this the end? Sam stared down at the envelope
in her hand. Did it hold a severance cheque, notice
of termination of her employment as a pilot with
him?

There was no name and address typed on it. Surely
if it was something official, that would have been
done. And why deliver it to her on Christmas day?
Personally?

Her mind was a mess of painful confusion. The
answer was inside the envelope, she told herself, so
open it. Her fingers tremulously carried out the mental order and slowly extracted the contents—thin
pages from a stationery pad, handwritten in blue biro.
She unfolded them, and was startled to see it was a
personal letter, dated weeks ago, with Kununurra
Hospital written under the date. Bewildered, and not
knowing what to expect, she started to read...

Dear Samantha,

Firstly, let me say how sorry I am to have
caused so much trouble and pain. My parents told

me it was you who flew them to the hospital on the night of the accident, and I appreciate that very much, especially since I'd been such a bitch to you earlier.

Janice... This was from Janice Findlay! Dazedly, Sam read on....

I'm writing this because I need to get it off my chest, and I owe it to you, too. You never did anything to hurt me and how can I make a fresh start if I don't clear my conscience? So here goes, and I hope you're still reading.

The truth is I lied about Tommy being the father of my baby. I guess getting pregnant made me face up to what a shambles my life was in. No, that's wrong. I didn't really face up to it. I kind of clutched at Tommy as the one really decent man I'd ever been with and hoped he would see me through.

He tried to steer me towards help when he broke off with me, but I just resented his advice and went off on a partying binge to forget him. One night I picked up a tourist and fell into bed with him. I couldn't even remember his name afterwards. That's how bad I'd got. Then when I found out I'd fallen pregnant, I panicked. I didn't want to tell my Mum and Dad I didn't even know the father's name.

I knew it wasn't right to try to pin it on Tommy, but by the time Nathan's wedding came around, I was seeing that as the only solution, and I kept telling myself it could have been his child, so it was fair. Although he had always used protection, I argued that nothing was a hundred percent safe so I could get past that. I just didn't bargain on you, and Tommy wanting you.

It completely threw me. I rocketed straight off to drink myself silly again and latch onto a guy who fancied me. I didn't deliberately pick your brother. Didn't even know he was your brother until we'd been chatting each other up for a while. Actually I did like Greg but life on the land is not for me.

Anyhow I really burned during the reception, seeing Tommy giving you all the attention I wanted from him. I tried to corner him when you slipped out of the marquee, but he fobbed me off on his brother, Jared, and went after you, which made me even madder.

Then I saw you both coming back, so very together, and your hair was down. I knew you'd been having sex, which meant my house of cards was tumbling all around me and I just went crazy. I guess, because I'd thought about it so much, I convinced myself Tommy was the father of my baby, doing the dirty on me, and I let you both have it because it felt like you'd taken him away from me.

I realise now how terribly wrong that was. Tommy wasn't mine. I had no claim on him at all. And you were a completely innocent party. I'm deeply ashamed of all my actions that night, hurting everyone, even killing the baby because I was so drunk and reckless and off my brain.

Well, it's pulled me up with a jolt, I can tell you. Not that it mends what I've done. I hope this letter goes some way towards fixing things between you and Tommy. Incidentally, Tommy didn't ask me to do this but I did tell him I was doing it because I wanted him to know I'm really trying to put things straight now.

He's been so kind since the accident, helping to explain things to Mum and Dad, making them see me as I am—if not an alcoholic, going that way fast—and very much in need of counselling and a lot of support to see me through it. I didn't deserve this from him. He says I'm worth saving for myself. I don't know how he can see any good in me after what I did, but I'm very grateful he's been here, holding my hand when I needed it.

I'm flying home with Mum and Dad tomorrow. Out of Tommy's life. Out of your life, too, Samantha. At least, I hope so. I hope I'm not going to leave a legacy of lies, spoiling things I had no right to spoil. I would like to think of you being happy with Tommy again, as happy as you looked that night before I stepped in and wrecked what I saw happening between you.

I'm so sorry.

Please smile at Tommy. He deserves it.

                                          Janice Findlay.

Sam couldn't smile. Her face was impossibly stiff, aching with the build up of tears that were beginning to swim into her eyes. She couldn't speak, either. The lump in her throat was so huge she could barely swallow.

Tommy had asked her to trust him. And she hadn't. She hadn't. She had believed the accusation against him, and multiplied it to even worse proportions, doing him a terrible injustice, turning him into much less than the decent man he was. How could she have got it so wrong, she who had known him all these years, most of her life, and knowing he always treated people well, knowing he was essentially fair-minded and generous of heart?

Except with her.

But hadn't that been her fault? And this was her fault, too. She'd made a habit of judging him meanly. The leaden weight on her heart grew heavier. Was it any use, asking him to forgive her? Would he give her another chance?

Her father's words slid through the dark anguish in her mind... *Christmas Day...peace and good will...* and a bare sliver of hope whispered—why would Tommy come today if he wanted to lay blame on her?

Slowly, almost blindly, she folded the pages of Janice's letter into its original creases. Please, she prayed. Please let Tommy be here because he still wants me, despite everything. She wasn't aware that the tears had overflowed and were rolling down her cheeks. She was only conscious of desperate need.

"Don't!"

The harsh command jerked her head up, fear jabbing through her that she'd done more wrong. Her vision was too blurred to see him clearly.

"Don't cry."

Not a command. A plea. Yet the difference barely had time to register before Tommy stepped forward and wrapped her in his arms, hugging her to him so tightly, there was no room left for fear. And her own arms wound around his waist, hanging on, hanging on for dear life.

Then his voice, throbbing into her ear, "Say you still want me." And the words lifting the weight off her heart, bringing such sweet relief, instantly drawing the reply, "I do. I do want you."

His kiss, his body, the pent-up passion pouring from him, left no doubt about what he felt. And Sam gave herself up to it, shedding all her fears and uncertainties, caring only that she have this...this blissful togetherness with Tommy.

Neither of them thought about ghosts.

There were none to come between them anymore.

CHAPTER FIFTEEN

"WILL YOU come with me?"

The passionate intensity of his kiss was echoed in Tommy's murmured words, and to Sam's giddy mind he was asking if she would travel with him on whatever path took them into a future together.

"Yes," she breathed fervently, not hesitating for a second.

She felt his chest heave with relief. Then in an action so swift it left her breathless and bewildered, he scooped her off her feet and had her firmly slung across that very same chest, her legs dangling over one of his arms while his other arm held her very securely to him.

"I'm taking you to a very special place," he stated, striding back towards the plane.

"You don't have to carry me," she assured him, although she happily wound her arms around his neck, loving his strength and the determined purpose that included her.

He grinned, his eyes dancing with devilish pleasure. "I like knowing I've got you."

She laughed and it was so good to laugh, to feel free and full of the joy of being alive. Over his shoulder, she caught sight of her family, still watching from the verandah, but it didn't matter what they

176

thought. They'd be happy for her, too, if they knew how much this meant.

"You haven't said hello to my family and I haven't said goodbye," she said, reminded of this oversight.

"We'll wave," came the unabashed reply.

Sam hitched herself up a bit to smile and wave at her parents and brothers. Greg flashed her a V for victory. Pete raised his arms above his head like a champion boxer. Her father held up a salute while gathering her mother close to him, hugging her shoulders. They were smiling at each other, prompting Sam to wonder how much they had talked about her and Tommy between themselves. It was very apparent her whole family was well pleased she was going off with him, and far from spoiling their Christmas day, it seemed to have topped it off very nicely. Which added to her sense of brilliant well-being.

Tommy bundled her into the cockpit and she wriggled over into the passenger seat, smiling to herself at the novelty of not being at the controls. Today she was not flying *for* Tommy King. She was flying *with* him, up into the wide blue sky and wherever he wanted to take her.

He waved to the Connelly family before climbing in and settling himself, ready for take-off. Before switching on the engine, he shot her a sharp, searching look. "Any questions?"

"No," she promptly replied. "None at all," she added emphatically, wanting to assert her intention never to lose faith in him and his feeling for her again.

He smiled, whatever inner reservations he'd held, wiped out in a burst of elation at her decisiveness. "No going back on that, Samantha Connelly. I won't let you," he warned.

Which instantly reminded her of the promise she'd made and hadn't kept, once Janice's claim had seemed ratified. "What about you, Tommy? Do you have any questions of me?" she asked gravely, impelled to probe how much of a scar her lack of trust had left on him.

The smile tilted into wry self-mockery. "How could you know my truth, when I've given you every reason to doubt it? Right now I'm feeling very lucky that you have such a constant heart, and I hope nothing I do will ever test it again."

"I'm sorry I..."

"No!" Silencing fingers on her lips and his eyes burning with intense resolution. "We're not going to do any more of that...looking back to what we did wrong. We've got it right now, haven't we?"

She nodded.

"There's a lot of life ahead of us, Samantha. Let's start from here. Okay?"

She nodded again, grateful for his understanding and the answering of her own hopes and needs.

He relaxed, flashing her another brilliant smile. "No clouds. Come fly with me."

"Yes," she happily agreed.

They flew to Kununurra where Tommy exchanged the plane for a helicopter from the KingAir charter service fleet and quickly grabbed some picnic supplies from the office. Her curiosity piqued, Sam asked him where they were going, but Tommy would only say it was a surprise. Since there was no mistaking the undercurrent of excitement in his manner, Sam reasoned the *special* place he had in mind, was very special to him, and she hoped it would have the same appeal to her. It would add so much more to the sense of sharing if it did.

It was a very short flight. They landed on a hill overlooking Lake Argyle which always looked fantastic—the largest manmade lake in Australia covering about two thousand square kilometres, and perfect for swimming, boating and fishing. The many bays and inlets and islands added an interesting landscape to the huge expanse of water, which definitely had a cooling effect on Outback heat—very welcome to Sam when she flew tourists here.

Though not exactly *here*. She had never landed on this hill. It wasn't a tourist place, which made it all the more attractive, having this lovely view to themselves. She smiled delightedly at Tommy as he finished laying a groundsheet under a nearby stand of gum trees so they could sit in the shade.

"Did you scout all the surrounds of the lake to find this hill?"

"More or less," he admitted.

"It's glorious, Tommy. Very special."

"I'm glad you think so because I chose it specially."

"What for?"

His eyes sparkled happy anticipation as he stepped

over to her and slid his arms around her waist. "This is my land, Samantha. I set about buying it soon after I found this place. To me, it was perfect for what I wanted."

She frowned, relating his planning to business. "Another tourist lodge?"

He shook his head and lifted a hand to smooth the lines from her forehead. His eyes smiled into hers as he warmly answered, "To build a home on. A home that would be here for me and my wife and my family."

Sam's heart turned over.

His fingers stroked gently down her face. "Would you be happy to share it with me, Samantha?"

"Yes," she whispered.

"To marry me and have my children?"

"Yes."

He sighed, a deep contentment in his eyes. "I shall love you all my life."

Sam didn't doubt that promise for a moment. Her hands slid up to link around his neck as she huskily answered, "And I you, Tommy. I you…always and forever."

And the words themselves—spoken, meant, felt—put all the magical reality of the future they wanted within tangible reach as they kissed and revelled in a totally uninhibited giving of each other. Clothes were discarded, the need to satisfy every sense of absolute union sizzling through them, and for a long, blissful time they lay on their hill, on the site of the home they would build together, making love with all the tenderness of caring, the elation of knowing, the fierce urge for mutual possession, the ecstasy of fulfilment, the sweet sensual contentment of peace and harmony.

Sunset...always an hour of relaxation at King's Eden, though Elizabeth wished Tommy was with them—Tommy and Sam. Nevertheless, it was very pleasant, sitting out here on the wicker furniture spread along the western verandah, sipping cool drinks and watching the river below them turning into a stream of gold.

The sound of a helicopter coming in jarred the peace and set Elizabeth's mind and heart racing.

"Tommy," Jared murmured.

"He flew off in a plane," Elizabeth reminded him.

"Yes. Interesting that he's returning in a helicopter."

No doubt in his voice about who the pilot was, coming in at dusk on Christmas Day. It had to be Tommy, Elizabeth conceded, and fiercely willed the change to a helicopter meant something positive.

"The question is...with or without Sam," Nathan remarked, speaking what was on all their minds.

No one commented. No one moved. There was nothing they could do, either way. Impossible for any of them to direct Tommy's life. Elizabeth knew they were all hoping his quest had been successful and he was bringing home his *gift of a lifetime,* but if he'd failed...well, he certainly wouldn't appreciate any open fuss about it.

They waited. The helicopter landed. The whirling clatter of its blades stopped. The ensuing silence stretched Elizabeth's nerves. She imagined Tommy trudging up to the homestead alone. Surely he would have stayed with the Connellys if...

Voices!

"That's Sam!" Jared said with certainty, his face breaking into a delighted grin. "He's got her!"

Elizabeth heaved a huge sigh of relief. This had to mean peace and good will, if nothing else.

"We're out here on the verandah, Tommy," Nathan called out, his voice booming with a big welcome. "Come join us!"

"Be right there!" came the happy reply. *Happy!*

Then quick and eager footsteps along the verandah, approaching the corner to the western side. Elizabeth put her glass down and leaned forward in her chair, her own eagerness to see and assess the situation brimming up in her. Tommy and Sam swung into view, hand in hand, their faces beaming so much joy there was no possible doubting they were in perfect harmony.

"This is most fortuitous!" Tommy declared. "Here you are all gathered precisely where Samantha and I shared our first kiss on Nathan's and Miranda's wedding day. Isn't that right, darling?"

She laughed, both nodding and shaking her head at him.

"And before anyone says anything," he went on, bubbling with obvious exhilaration. "Let me introduce my future wife..." He halted, turned and tenderly cupped Sam's face, bringing her gaze directly in line with his. "...who will truly be to me..." his voice dropped to a warm caress of love "…the most beautiful bride in the whole world."

Tears glistened in Sam's eyes. Elizabeth sensed those words meant a great deal to the woman she had always been inside, the woman who had wanted Tommy to recognise and love her. Now the love was so evident Elizabeth found tears pricking her own eyes.

Her heart was so full, she was the last to get up to congratulate them on their forthcoming marriage. Jared, Nathan, Miranda…all of them swarmed around the newly announced couple, hugging, laughing, showing their pleasure. Finally she was on her feet, joining the others.

"Mum…" Tommy grinned at her, his eyes dancing wickedly. "…it really goes against the grain for me, at my age, to say *Mother knows best*, but I'll grant it this time."

"And I do, too," Sam agreed, her lovely blue eyes sparkling with appreciation.

Elizabeth gestured helplessly, realising they were both acknowledging her words to them before Nathan's wedding. "It was always up to you two," she reminded them. "I just can't tell you how pleased I am that you finally found each other."

That was the truth of it. She might have prodded them a little, but it had still been their choice to open their hearts and minds to each other. And thank heaven they had!

Much, much later when the homestead was quiet, Elizabeth lay in the bed she had once shared with Lachlan, counting the blessings of this Christmas and feeling very content with the way the future was shaping—two sons married to women who were surely their soul mates, one grandchild on the way.

If she could see Jared similarly settled... Was Christabel Valdez the right woman? Would the enigmatic Brazilian ever open her heart to him? Was there anything she herself could do to foster a clearer situation between them? Or should she let that relationship fly all by itself?

Elizabeth sighed and settled herself for sleep. Today, all was well at King's Eden. Lachlan would have been so pleased and proud. And Jared was the youngest son. His time would come, too, she told herself, with or without Christabel Valdez. It had been a good year. A very good year. Nathan and Miranda and the baby, Tommy and Sam. No need to worry about Jared.

The family would go on...future generations...the Kings of the Outback...Lachlan's heritage safe. She could rest in peace tonight. She no longer felt the gnawing sense of loss that had driven her from King's Eden. It wasn't just the past here now. It held a future, as well.

Author's Note

THE STORY you have just read is the second of three
revolving around the Kings of the Kimberly—all of
them set in the Outback of Australia.

I trust you have enjoyed reading how Tommy
King and Samantha Connelly finally came together
in "The Playboy King's Wife."

I hope you will be intrigued by Christabel's story
and eager to read how the third King brother, Jared,
pursues his passion for this enigmatic woman in *The
Pleasure King's Bride*. This title will be available in
the coming months and I promise you surprises and
atisfaction in this last book of my Outback trilogy.

Emma Darcy

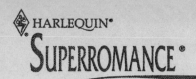
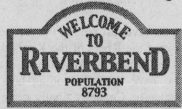

If you enjoyed what you just read,
then we've got an offer you can't resist!

Take 2 bestselling
love stories FREE!
Plus get a FREE surprise gift!

Romance is just one click away!

online book **serials**

➤ *Exclusive* to our web site, get caught up in both the daily and weekly online installments of new romance stories.

➤ Try the Writing Round Robin. Contribute a chapter to a story created by our members. Plus, winners will get prizes.

romantic **travel**

➤ Want to know where the best place to kiss in New York City is, or which restaurant in Los Angeles is the most romantic? Check out our Romantic Hot Spots for the scoop.

➤ Share your travel tips and stories with us on the romantic travel message boards.

romantic reading **library**

➤ Relax as you read our collection of Romantic Poetry.

➤ Take a peek at the Top 10 Most Romantic Lines!

Visit us online at

www.eHarlequin.com
on Women.com Networks

HARLEQUIN *Presents*

Set in the steamy Australian outback
a fabulous new triology by
bestselling Presents author

Emma Darcy

Kings of the
Outback

Three masterful brothers
and the women who tame them

On sale June 2000
THE CATTLE KING'S MISTRESS
Harlequin Presents®, #2110

On sale July 2000
THE PLAYBOY KING'S WIFE
Harlequin Presents®, #2116

On sale August 2000
THE PLEASURE KING'S BRIDE
Harlequin Presents®, #2122

Available wherever Harlequin books are sold.

HARLEQUIN®
Makes any time special™

Visit us at www.eHarlequin.com

HPKING

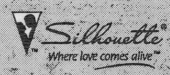

Coming Next Month

THE BEST HAS JUST GOTTEN BETTER!

#2121 THE ITALIAN'S REVENGE Michelle Reid
Vito Giordani had never forgiven Catherine for leaving, and now, seizing the advantage, he demanded that she return to Naples with him—as his wife. Their son would have his parents back together—and Vito would finally have...revenge!

#2122 THE PLEASURE KING'S BRIDE Emma Darcy
Fleeing from a dangerous situation, Christabel Valdez can't afford to fall in love. But she can't resist one night of passion with Jared King. And will one night be enough...?

#2123 HIS SECRETARY BRIDE
Kim Lawrence and Cathy Williams
(2-in-1 anthology)
From boardroom...to bedroom. What should you do if your boss is a gorgeous, sexy man and you simply can't resist him? Find out in these two lively, emotional short stories by talented rising stars Kim Lawrence and Cathy Williams.

#2124 OUTBACK MISTRESS Lindsay Armstrong
Ben had an accident on Olivia's property and had briefly lost his memory. Olivia couldn't deny the chemistry between them—but two vital discoveries turned her against him....

#2125 THE UNMARRIED FATHER Kathryn Ross
Melissa had agreed to pose as Mac's partner to help him secure a business contract. But after spending time with him and his adorable baby daughter, Melissa wished their deception could turn into reality....

#2126 RHYS'S REDEMPTION Anne McAllister
Rhys Wolfe would never risk his heart again. He cared about Mariah, but they were simply good friends. Their one night of passion had been a mistake. Only, now Mariah was pregnant—and Rhys had just nine months to learn to trust in love again.

CNM0700